CRUISIN' FOR LOVE

SEAL Brotherhood: Legacy Series
Book 5

SHARON HAMILTON

D1595642

SHARON HAMILTON'S BOOK LIST

SEAL BROTHERHOOD BOOKS

SEAL BROTHERHOOD SERIES
Accidental SEAL Book 1

Fallen SEAL Legacy Book 2

SEAL Under Covers Book 3

SEAL The Deal Book 4

Cruisin' For A SEAL Book 5

SEAL My Destiny Book 6

SEAL of My Heart Book 7

Fredo's Dream Book 8

SEAL My Love Book 9

SEAL Encounter Prequel to Book 1

SEAL Endeavor Prequel to Book 2

Ultimate SEAL Collection Vol. 1 Books 1-4 /2 Prequels

Ultimate SEAL Collection Vol. 2 Books 5-7

SEAL BROTHERHOOD LEGACY SERIES
Watery Grave Book 1

Honor The Fallen Book 2

Grave Injustice Book 3

Deal With The Devil Book 4

Cruisin' For Love Book 5

BAD BOYS OF SEAL TEAM 3 SERIES
SEAL's Promise Book 1
SEAL My Home Book 2
SEAL's Code Book 3
Big Bad Boys Bundle Books 1-3

BAND OF BACHELORS SERIES
Lucas Book 1
Alex Book 2
Jake Book 3
Jake 2 Book 4
Big Band of Bachelors Bundle

BONE FROG BROTHERHOOD SERIES
New Year's SEAL Dream Book 1
SEALed At The Altar Book 2
SEALed Forever Book 3
SEAL's Rescue Book 4
SEALed Protection Book 5
Bone Frog Brotherhood Superbundle

BONE FROG BACHELOR SERIES
Bone Frog Bachelor Book 0.5
Unleashed Book 1
Restored Book 2
Revenge Book 3
Legacy Book 4

Paradise: In Search of Love
Love Me Tender, Love You Hard

NOVELLAS
SEAL You In My Dreams Magnolias and Moonshine

PARANORMALS

GOLDEN VAMPIRES OF TUSCANY SERIES
Honeymoon Bite Book 1
Mortal Bite Book 2
Christmas Bite Book 3
Midnight Bite Book 4

THE GUARDIANS
Heavenly Lover Book 1
Underworld Lover Book 2
Underworld Queen Book 3
Redemption Book 4

FALL FROM GRACE SERIES
Gideon: Heavenly Fall

NOVELLAS
SEAL Of Time Trident Legacy

All of Sharon's books are available on Audible,
narrated by the talented J.D. Hart.

ABOUT THE BOOK

Mark Beale and his wife, Sophia, plan to celebrate ten years of marriage by going on a trans-Atlantic cruise from Italy to the Caribbean at Christmas with their three daughters. Hoping to erase the memories of past cruises which turned out to be complete disasters, they plan to renew their wedding vows, enjoy a relaxing family vacation, and visit Sophia's mother in Italy.

But for this Navy SEAL and his family, will the third time be the charm, or will they be unlucky again? Why does danger threaten to not only ruin their cruise, but their family?

Enjoy appearances by Captain Teseo Dominichello and other characters from SEAL Team 3.

Readers should enjoy reading Cruisin' For A SEAL first, the story of how Mark and Sophia met years ago. This book is a continuation of their relationship and the growth of their family after ten years have passed.

AUTHOR'S NOTE

I always dedicate my SEAL Brotherhood books to the brave men and women who defend our shores and keep us safe. Without their sacrifice, and that of their families—because a warrior's fight always includes his or her family—I wouldn't have the freedom and opportunity to make a living writing these stories. They sometimes pay the ultimate price so we can debate, argue, go have coffee with friends, raise our children and see them have children of their own.

One of my favorite tributes to warriors resides on many memorials, including one I saw honoring the fallen of WWII on an island in the Pacific:

> "When you go home
> Tell them of us, and say
> For your tomorrow,
> We gave our today."

These are my stories created out of my own imagination. Anything that is inaccurately portrayed is either my mistake, or done intentionally to disguise something I might have overheard over a beer or in the corner of one of the hangouts along the Coronado Strand.

I support two main charities. Navy SEAL/UDT Museum operates in Ft. Pierce, Florida. Please learn about this wonderful museum, all run by active and former SEALs and their friends and families, and who rely on public support, not that of the U.S. Government. www.navysealmuseum.org

IF YOU GOT ANY CLOSER, YOU WOULD HAVE TO ENLIST

I also support Wounded Warriors, who tirelessly bring together the warrior as well as the family members who are just learning to deal with their soldicr's condition and have nowhere to turn. It is a long path to becoming well, but I've seen first-hand what this organization does for its warriors and the families who love them. Please give what your heart tells you is right. If you cannot give, volunteer at one of the many service centers all over the United States. Get involved. Do something meaningful for someone who gave so much of themselves, to families who have paid the price for your freedom. You'll find a family there unlike any other on the planet. www.woundedwarriorproject.org

CHAPTER 1

Mark Beale entered his small galley kitchen, cartoons playing in the background. The girls had awakened him again, just like they did every Saturday morning, no matter if he was just returning from a deployment the night before or not.

He was wearing a pair of shorts, but no T-shirt, and was barefoot. His wife, Sophia, was reading a newspaper and had her hair flopped on top of her head, secured with a big clip, dark curly strands running all down the back of her neck and shoulders. Her peach-colored nightie was gaping in front. The nightie was well used, slightly frayed, and hopelessly stained where she had spilled coffee in previous days.

Mark remembered giving it to Sophia on their anniversary some nearly ten years ago.

How things change.

But then he looked down at himself with his bare feet, wrinkled boxers, and sleep crust clinging to both eyes. He could have said something but chose to just reach for the coffee and overlook that part.

Sophia didn't say a word and didn't look up at him, just like his girls had done as he passed them on his trek to the kitchen for his cup of Joe.

He moved aside the pickles, the lime yogurts, and almond milk to find his coveted heavy whipping cream, which was as important to his morning routine as the coffee.

"Well, would you look at us, honey?" he said to his wife.

That's when Sophia did manage to get a good look at him. "Whatever do you mean?"

"Aren't we a pair? Did you ever think when we got married some ten years ago that we would be spending Saturday morning looking like this?"

He demonstrated on himself first and then motioned to her with a stylish gesture.

"I did not."

She was rather blunt. Okay, he could have expected that.

"And instead of elevator music or Italian romantic songs playing in the promenades and hallways of the cruise ships, we'd be listening to Sesame Street and Mr. Buck on the TV? Not to mention the dog channel or the Cockapoo station."

"You're complaining now? Is that what's going on

now?"

He should have answered he discovered too late.

"Mark, maybe it's just as simple as not getting laid enough?"

God help him for her frankness, the way she just skewered him with the look of her eyes, the little flippant comments she made in Italian—sometimes under her breath, her haughty attitude, and her vivaciousness. She exuded confidence over the table, even when she was in her nightie, her *stained* nightie, and had been up half the night with their youngest, Domenica.

"So, it was a tough night for you?" he asked her. "Sorry about that, but thanks for letting me sleep a little at least."

"My fault then?"

"Don't start with me. I woke up to the sound of the TV blaring, and you know, I got in last night at two o'clock. I like to sleep in on Saturdays. It's always been like this, at least since the children came. With babies, even without babies. Before I got married and all ten years since we got married. It was even like this on the cruise ship. Remember?"

"How could I forget? The mysterious man coming back from missions all hours of the night, his need for sex so strong we could fuck for six hours afterwards. But no, now you come home and sleep for a day and a half. And what about the sex? You know, Mark, I have needs as well."

Mark knew it wouldn't be very smart to mention something about her appearance. Especially as he realized his own appearance looked far from sexy or masculine or warrior-type. Yes, he had tattoos, he had some scars, and he certainly had muscles, including six pack abs and biceps. He knew that even though she was shorter and weighed half what he did, he would pay dearly for that comment. He kept it to himself and decided to finish his coffee.

"You're just gonna leave it like that?" she asked him.

"I am." It was Mark's turn to be smug.

"What are you saying exactly?"

"Nothing, just that your nightie reminded me of the fact that there are anniversaries, and there are people who celebrate them. I just thought that since we're going to have a ten-year coming up here soon, that we could do something special for it. Maybe take the kids to Disneyland or some other thing? How about camping?"

Sophia looked over the newspaper like he was wearing the contents of Domenica's dirty diaper.

"So, I'm open to suggestions now. This is me being flexible, being awake, and asking you what you would like to do for your anniversary?"

Sophia sighed heavily, looking down at the paper rattling between her hands, letting her feet tap on the floor, which was something Mark had discovered was common amongst dancers, and impatiently returned an answer he didn't expect.

"I'd like you to surprise me. Do something spontaneous, dangerous!"

"Can you give me a hint?"

"Then that wouldn't be spontaneous." Sophia shook her head from side to side. "No."

Mark knew better than to walk on thin ice, and the kitchen certainly had lots of thin ice. "What do you think the kids would like to do?"

"I thought you said this is for our anniversary?"

"Dammit, Sophia, this *is* for our anniversary. But are you thinking about leaving them somewhere?"

"I guess that's out of the question then. My mistake." She was getting frostier by the minute.

He knew that, in very short order, she was going to be suggesting that perhaps they could spend their anniversary apart, and since it was Christmas, she might make an exit to Italy to visit her mother, who had been failing health-wise. He didn't like the idea of it, and, if he could stop her from doing this, he certainly would try his darndest.

He poured himself another cup of coffee, adding more cream, asking her if she'd like a refill, which she declined. Grabbing his mug, he sat at a forty-five-degree angle to her at the table. Putting his chin in his left palm, his elbow on the table, in his best masculine, sexy voice, he said, "Sophia, the love of my life, the mother of my insanely beautiful daughters, who are the most spectacular little girls in the whole world, I want to do something that is *special* for you. I'd like to do something that would excite you, and I'd like to do something the kids would like as well. I don't even care if it's something like going to ballet camp because I'll do anything. I just want to do something that doesn't cost too much money, but something that we can do as a family, to celebrate our family after ten years. It's gone by so fast, and I'm gone so much of the time, that it would be really a good idea if we could try to do a family vacation. All of us together!"

At first, he waited for her answer. Her eyes studied him, moving from his right eye to his left eye and back to his right, examining the stubble on his chin, then following the trail of chest hair down lower, making him swallow with a parched mouth. He was hoping that was a good sign. He certainly *needed* a good sign right about now.

And then she folded the paper up in front of her, lacing her fingers together, and waited again.

"Sophia? Well?"

"I think we should take a trip to Italy. Take the girls

to see their grandma. What about that?"

"Well, it's Christmas time, and the flights to Italy are going to be outrageously expensive. It's November. No deals this time of year. I just am not sure whether we can afford to do that right now, with your studio closing. I mean, we could max out our credit cards, but is that smart? It's Christmas."

"Exactly, it's Christmas. We can go as a family for our family Christmas present."

He thought about this for a while and knew that Mrs. Negri lived in a very tiny apartment over the meat market. He also knew that there was no way all five of them could fit there, so it would involve renting a hotel room, a car, and other things. As he started to add up the numbers, his stomach began to tumble a bit, not just from the coffee, but from the understanding that he was looking at a vacation that was easily going to cost him about ten grand. And he didn't have it in his bank account.

But giving up was not an option.

"I'll tell you what, I'll go to the bank today, and I'll see if they'll give me a small loan for the vacation. Maybe then we could pay for it on an installment type basis, not use the expensive credit cards. How about that?"

"OK."

Little Ophelia their middle daughter, who was seven years old, entered the kitchen, asking for some breakfast.

"Would you like cereal this morning or would you like some eggs?"

"Pancakes," she blurted out stubbornly.

"OK, but your daddy's gonna go to the store to get a few things that I'm missing. Why don't we have cereal today, and then tomorrow we can have the pancakes."

Mark watched as Ophelia protruded her lower lip as she so often did on just about every occasion when she wasn't going to be getting her way. He fully saw in his young daughter his wife's spirit and personality. He imagined that Sophia probably was just like her when she was young.

It was no wonder Mark felt trapped. He was surrounded by his women.

And he loved them all to the ends of the earth.

BY MONDAY MORNING, Sophia had arranged their trip, through the cruise ship she used to work for, which had several unblocked bookings that were bargains at nearly seventy-five percent of the original price. She even signed up to be a tour director, and part-time dance instructor, requesting a paid position for Mark to be her co-instructor as well. The arrangement would nearly pay their expenses in full. The airfare was included in the price, and there were slots available for the cruise over Christmas, so the girls wouldn't miss more than a few days of school. The cruise would originate in Naples, and after a stop in the Caribbean, would arrive in Miami.

The girls were delighted with the plans, calling their grandmother in Italy to spread the good news. Mark double-checked the schedule and was given some leeway to return a few days late.

So, on a windy, light rain day in San Diego, all five of them boarded their flight to Italy for their anniversary vacation. Sophia dressed all three of the girls in red dresses, and, for the first time in weeks, began to allow a smile to creep into her expression.

Mark knew that the two other cruises he'd been on were just unlucky happenstances, and the odds were in their favor for a smooth, relaxing family trip well out of harm's way. He wasn't going to let his teammates spook him, either.

Earlier, when he'd announced their plans and the reason for his absence, he withstood the catcalls from the Team during their meetings and workouts, where Fredo and Cooper especially rubbed in everything they could throw at him.

"Terrorists, they got terrorists in North Africa, and you'll be going right around the bulge, Mark. You remember the Canaries? The Azores? Morocco?"

Fredo teased. "You want to show your girls cobras and have your wife kidnapped to become someone's third wife?"

"Shut up, you asshole. That's not going to happen."

"Yeah, but you got to admit, SEAL Team 3 has bad luck when it comes to ocean voyages," added Cooper. "Somehow, if there's something going on, we seem to get right in the middle of it."

"Now, God wouldn't do that to me. After the first one, and then the redo to bury Gunny, he wouldn't put me in that boat," insisted Mark. "Besides, I *earned* a nice vacation with my lovely wife. She's so grateful she's going to get to see her mother she might stop making me clean up the dishes. I'm earning brownie points, gents. Not to worry there. My future looks bright, and I can't wait to have it all!"

"Well," Cooper said with his quiet drawl and tall-drink-of-water-stance, "Let's hope the God of Navy SEALs has a heart. All that rocking and rolling. You guys might as well try for number four!"

"Hey, don't push it, Coop. I'm not sure that's luck. Three is a good number, and I'm never complaining about that again."

"Ah, you're probably right, Mark. Besides, you two would have to be bent over the railing and keeping it quiet with all those girls, and you know they'll be watching you guys. Just make sure you don't fall overboard. Those ships don't turn on a dime."

Mark brushed it off. No way in Hell was he going to be bobbing up and down in the Atlantic Ocean by himself.

Just no fuckin' way.

CHAPTER 2

SOPHIA'S MOTHER LIVED on a tiny, winding street above an Italian meat market, several blocks off the city square, a little sub-shopping center of the town of Naples. The district was known as the Artesian District, something about an artesian well that had probably dried up during Roman times, but that was what it was called, the buildings built nearly four hundred years ago.

The village was known for its charm and quaint architecture with small archways over windows and doors, front stoops made of a solid block of granite or marble, well-worn into a U pattern, as if it was a soft pillow that had been stepped on.

The smells of the city were welcoming to her, not bested by the smells of the neighborhood, where some of the best butchers and pastry makers in Italy lived. There was a huge training center for hotel chefs, in an extravagant 15th century villa, surrounded by vineyards and fresh herb and flower gardens. The whole area in this district was magical, appearing with its apricot-orange glow to the land. The burnt umber reflection of the buildings on the sidewalk and other buildings, also reflected in the faces of the people as they hurried past.

It was a rainy day, and Sophia did her best to keep the girls holding hands single file, with the other end being manned by Mark. Of course, little Domenica couldn't walk for more than ten or fifteen minutes before she needed to be carried, and that was Mark's job. He also carried her computer case, his computer case, and a carry-on for the girls. Each of the older two had a small fuzzy animal backpack carrying all their activity projects while on the plane, plus a change of clothes.

As they wandered through the cobblestone walkway approaching her mother's apartment, Mark turned to her and gave her a sexy smile.

"Now it all comes back to me, Sophia." He bent over to explain to Ophelia and Carrie Ann with loving patience. "Your mother and I met on a little street just like this. That day she was having lunch with her mother in the piazza. You remember that sweetheart?"

"Where did you have that lunch?" Asked Ophelia. "I want to see it."

"It wasn't here, it was in Genoa. But a very similar

village. Mother moved here to Naples to be closer to her specialist. And she has several close friends in the area as well."

In fact, one of the things Sophia was going to check on was what kind of a job her brother and sister-in-law were doing taking care of their mother, since the sole responsibility for doing so was on their shoulders, not on Sophia's. But Mark and Sophia contributed to the fund where they could, which kept her mother playing bingo, bocce ball, and allowed her an occasional aid to accompany her to the markets. But more and more, she was confined to the apartment, and seldom left unless it was for a special occasion.

She had not seen her mother's new apartment, but had seen pictures that her brother, Paolo, had sent, and he gave her a FaceTime video of all the shops nearby where she could hop downstairs and make a quick purchase if she felt so inclined. She was now letting others do the errands for her.

"I think this is it, Mark." She spoke. The window of the meat market in front of them had several hanging plucked birds, sausages and salamis of every size and color, with a healthy customer line feeding out onto the roadway.

"Yes, it looks like it's the green door to the right of the glass front. Did I get the number?"

"I think so. Ring the doorbell."

That got the two older girls' attention. "I want to do it!" shouted Carrie Ann. She soon was arguing with her sister.

Mark knelt and whispered to both his girls, "Let's push the button at the same time, okay? And you both can greet grandma when she answers, how about that?"

"Okay."

As they pressed the smooth black button, a scratchy crackling sound came over the radio. "Hello?" Said a very faint and raspy older woman's voice.

"Hi, grandma!" Both girls said exuberantly.

"Ah, belle bambini! I am most pleased you have come to visit. You are early, no? I will buzz and you will enter, girls."

"Hi, mom," inserted Sophia. "Yes, we're all here. Do you need anything first before we come up?"

"No, dear, I'm all prepared. I've baked you some light dinner. Just prepared a little something, not much."

Sophia stepped back and rolled her eyes creasing her forehead. It was her signal that Mark picked up on immediately, her mother had probably stayed up very late for two nights in a row making homemade pasta and anything else she could muster, since it was a sacrilege for anyone to leave her home without being totally stuffed to the gills.

The buzzer sounded and Mark quickly turned the

handle and carried the little one upstairs, rehoisting the computer cases over his shoulder again, bringing the handled bag as well. The girls noisily clop clopped up the stairs like young horses. Sophia made sure that the door downstairs was closed and locked behind her. At the top of the landing, she began to smell that glorious olive oil, tomato and basil combination that was almost like apple pie to an American. That familiar scent of good home cooking and that regardless of what else was going on in the outside world, everything that was going to happen in the kitchen, would be ample, warm, extremely tasty, and filling.

She found her mother's appearance quite changed. Sophia was taken aback at the arc of her mother's upper spine, causing her to bend down and strain to look up to anything taller than about five feet. She had thinned out quite a bit, and her fingers contained swollen joints of arthritis, her movements were shaky and not graceful, and her voice was cut to half the decibels it usually was, very raspy and almost like she had a chronic smoker's cough. She was not a smoker, but her body was suffering from several ailments including a mild case of emphysema and high blood pressure. But she had aged probably twenty years in the last five years since Sophia and Mark last visited her.

Even with her bowed and frail body, she relished

the hugs from her grandchildren, even the little one, Domenica, coming up and grabbing granny's knees with both her arms nearly to the point of causing her to lose her balance. Mark helped his mother-in-law and helped maneuver the group into her tiny living room overlooking the cobblestone street, a small blue sliver of the Mediterranean visible beyond the town.

"Mm-mm, I have been dreaming of this kind of aroma for weeks and weeks. Mom, I think you outdid yourself again." Mark said.

"Well, son, this is a very special day. I have not met this little one here, Domenica, named after me I understand, is that correct?"

She was holding the baby who reached out and tried to grab her glasses but got a clump of graying hair instead. That wasn't going to stop the baby, who continued to poke at and pinch all sorts of things from the buttonhole on her sweater to the edge of her collar where she had tiny flowers embroidered along the collar's edge, the safety pins she wore in her hair, and the gold-rimmed spectacles she wore which flashed in the sunshine and was just pure eye candy to Domenica. She was desperately looking to get into trouble.

"Here, mom, I'm going to take her. She's a real handful. I'll wait till you're seated and then we can perhaps have her sit on your lap. That's probably safer."

Her mother didn't argue.

"Well, you come here and have a seat, girls. We have a nice table set for you and I put out all the crystal and the silver. I have your little cups here; I don't know if you remember I bought them when each of you were born. This is yours, Ophelia, and this is yours, Carrie Ann, and I even have a small stainless-steel cup for Domenica." She held up the tiny cup and Domenica, understanding that it probably belonged to her, reached out and was able to grab it before anyone could stop her.

Mrs. Negri chuckled, pressing her palms together as if in prayer. "She is so willful, just like her mother. I'm sure you've noticed, Mark."

"Actually, mom, they all have her spirit. They are little hurricanes in progress, tornadoes, every room they go through is destroyed. We are a very active family, and it's hard to keep up with them sometimes. I think I get more exhausted playing with the girls than I do working."

Sophia knew it was an exaggeration, but she didn't mind. She was basking in the glow of her aging mother's countenance, the kind woman who raised her, cared for her under very difficult circumstances when her American pilot father was killed, and she never remarried. She lived a very simple life, taking several jobs at once, and allowing Sophia to go to dance and music school, which worked very well as a glori-fied daycare setup for her and her jobs. Sophia was filled with pride at how she bore her simple life and had never heard her complain or be angry at anyone, except for herself. And her brother.

Just as she'd expected, the dinner was huge. She made cannelloni, chicken cacciatore, her favorite lobster raviolis with the scallop cream sauce. She had put together a pear currant and fresh lettuce salad with lots of grated Parmesan cheese and a thin oil and vinegar dressing that Sophia had not been able to recreate, even though the ingredients were so simple. They drank two bottles of wine, her mother nearly finishing off one all by herself. This surprised her, as it was a new occurrence.

"So, are you being well taken care of? Is there any-thing you need?" She asked her mother.

"I'm fine. I don't get out to see my friends as much anymore, and I have a young girl that comes to wash and cut my hair every other week. She is learning to be a hair stylist, but she's not passed her exams yet. She also helps me do some house cleaning when I feel up to it."

"Do you see Raphael and Julia?"

"No, my dear, I have not. Your cousins are very busy. I only see Paolo on certain occasions, but he telephones me. And we have a good chat now and

19

then."

"So, how often do you see the doctor?"

"I go every three months, for a checkup, I have a monitor that I wear, that reports directly to my doctor. It gives him all sorts of information including my pulse, so in case I am in a danger zone, they can send an ambulance. It's quite a handy thing. But I think the worst part of living alone and being this age is not having friends. The television has never been something I enjoy, and I can't figure out how to work my computer or my cell phone. Some of my friends do, but I don't. I prefer to read."

"I actually think that's better for you, mom." Mark added. "They say, reading and playing games, as well as walking, some little exercise at least, is what keeps you young. I think you're doing all the right things. And if you eat well, take your medications, I think you could go quite a while without any serious complications. Don't strain yourself, don't stand on ladders, and don't try to go down those stairs by yourself, those are awfully steep and tiny."

"But I am a size four shoe, Mark. The stairs are no problem for me with the handrails on both sides. I glide down those stairs almost like a fire pole at a station." She gave Mark one of those loving smiles that Sophia imagined the Virgin Mary might have looked in one of the frescoes in several of the churches they attended as she was growing up. Her mother was the picture of peace.

"That's good to hear, mom." Said Sophia.

"Why don't the girls go sit in the living room, I can bring out some cards," she said without asking permission. "How about playing cards the two of you?"

The girls agreed and Mrs. Negri went to the cabinet and brought out a deck of cards with kittens on the backside. The girls were more interested in pictures of the kittens than they were setting up their card game.

Mrs. Negri returned to the table and sat down with a grunt. "Sophia, I am slowing down. And I really don't know how long I will be here. I do not want to be a burden. They do have state facilities here in Italy, but I don't want to be housed in one of those places. I would prefer to live with Paolo and his wife, but they have no room. Do you suppose, if I could pay for the plane fare, that someday when the time came, I could live with you in California?"

Mark's eyes got as big as saucers. Sophia knew he was wondering where the heck she would stay, and yes that more than likely he was making a private joke to himself that she might have to sleep in the Land Rover since there would be no room in their tiny house.

He spoke up immediately. "Our place is not much bigger than this apartment, mom. We have two bedrooms, all three of the girls stay together, and Sophia and I have the other."

"Oh, I don't mind, I can sleep just fine on a couch."

Mark leaned into the table and with his right hand put it on top of Mrs. Negri's gnarled fingers maintaining a knot on the tablecloth beneath. "Mom, if you want to come live with us in California, we'll make it work. Somehow, we'll make it work. I'm not sure whether this house would work, but perhaps we can find something that would be bigger. We live a very simple life, but I would be honored if you'd come live with us, and the girls would get to know their grandmother. I think it would be wonderful. In fact, I'm going to consider it my anniversary present. *Please* come. You are more than welcome."

Sophia's eyes filled with tears. She had never seen or heard anything so beautiful coming from Mark's mouth before. She held her mother's hand with Mark's on her left side and reached out for Mark's other hand with her right.

The three of them formed a perfect circle.

CHAPTER 3

THE SHIP TERMINAL in Napoli was a complete zoo. They had spent two relaxing days with Sophia's mother, taking her shopping, getting her ready for Christmas, and exchanging little gifts, mostly for the girls. But transitioning from the little sleepy village she lived in, to the boat terminal with the masses of international population, was quite an adjustment.

There were four cruise ships docked, and each terminal had a staged embarkation setup, to try to mitigate traffic. But this being Italy, Mark was extremely familiar with how delivery vehicles, tour operators, and the general European public did things so he knew it would be a complete clusterfuck.

He didn't mind large crowds when he was doing surveillance for an upcoming op. He could blend into the audience and watch certain people, because he was generally targeting specific individuals rather than the crowd. That was an unmanageable thing to do. He would never do well trying to run a massive exodus of tourists from all over the world, no matter how patient or skilled he was in communication.

But it was different when his natural training as a SEAL, made him suspicious of absolutely every person in the terminal. He was uncomfortable because he was not allowed to be near a doorway or a window for a speedy exit in case of an emergency event. He was smack in the center, waiting in line, and, even if he wanted to bolt, it would be impossible without climbing over old ladies, children, dogs, and porters with huge carts piled high with luggage.

It was claustrophobic, hot and sweaty. The tour operators were trying to keep their buses of passengers together, holding signs above their heads and screaming in their language of choice. Since this cruise was going to stop in several countries that bordered the Mediterranean, including France and Spain, there were passengers arriving on board who would be leaving the next day or two. It was more like a ferry terminal than an actual cruise ship embarkation.

By the time they made their way through the line up to the final immigration desk, Mark's neck was sore from whipping around, watching every loud shout or event, a dropped bag or something that would resemble in any way a gunshot. He was packing, which was allowed, if he went through proper channels and showed his credentials. That was one thing Sophia managed to verify before she even placed the reservation, because cruise ship rules had changed significantly since the onset of COVID, as well as the increase in international piracy at sea.

On top of the noise, the congestion, and the sheer abundance of humanity, half the passengers were wearing masks, and half were not. Identification was nearly impossible, and he knew that people who had nefarious reputations were using that to the highest effectiveness.

They were asked several questions. The handsome Italian gentleman in his uniform even had medals adorning his outfit, including a ten-year pin, and a bunch of brassy epaulets on both shoulders made with spun golden braid. He was trim, had a neatly trimmed mustache, his warm brown eyes lovingly caressed every single beautiful woman he encountered, as well as the children. And when he perused Mark, he gave a distracted, utterly bored, and very cool stare.

"Everything is in order, sir. I bid you good day, and I hope you enjoy your cruise," The gentleman said, handing Mark the stack of passports. Sophia had Dominica's picture with her passport, but each of the girls, Ophelia, and Carrie Ann, had their own passports.

They walked up the gangway way behind the two

girls, who were hopping like bunnies, holding up the entire line of people anxious to get to their cabins. He moved aside to allow others to go around him, which earned him a couple slaps in the thigh with luggage, computer cases, and in one case a barking Lhasa Apso in a pink sequined hard case.

They approached a landing before entering the ship, where the obligatory photo was to be taken with two clown characters. The first clown had bright red hair, with a fully painted up Edgar Gacy-style. Next to him stood a female ship's captain with disheveled uniform and wrinkled tie lopping off over her shoulder. She had smudge marks on her face, dressed up in caricature as a drunken officer of the ship.

Mark thought it was an odd way to help people feel comfortable about their crews. He hated clowns and knew Sophia did as well.

But the girls didn't care and even though Mark heard Sophia groan, they ran to the clowns and stood in front of them beaming wide for the camera.

The photographer, a big man with a squeaky voice addressed them both. "Come, come. Mom, Dad? Come, we can't have you out of the photo. You must come." The photographer barked like a huckster.

"But you have the pictures of the girls. That's all we want," said Sophia.

"No, no, no. You do not have to buy, but it is a rule

we must take your whole picture as a family."

Resigned to it, Mark put his aviators back on, which served as an ample disguise, and stood with his hand on his wife's shoulder, his other hand on Carrie Ann's shoulder in front of him and smiled, showing his freshly cleaned teeth.

There was a flurry of Italian spoken by both clowns and the photographer fussing about straightening the girls' dresses and smoothing down their hair, and for Mark's taste, got a little too close to Sophia.

Sophia was right on it.

"Excuse me? I didn't give you permission to touch me or my children. And besides, I am staff." Sophia dug in her day bag finding her badge for the two of them and held them up not more than two inches from the photographer's eyeballs. "Understand?"

"Si. Si, si, signora. We are almost finished. One more picture. Please." He had his hands together. His head bowed slightly as if he was truly begging for forgiveness.

She grabbed the girls by their arms and whispered, "Goddammit, next time we just walk right past it, okay? It'll be like this at every single port of call. They'll make you go in front of the dancers or the musicians, the handcrafts or whatever. No more pictures, Mark. Okay? Can you help me with that?"

"Absolutely, sweetheart."

Next, they picked up their packet from the information desk, and taking turns Sophia and Mark entered the employee only area, leaving the other to watch the girls, picking up their informational packet and checking their medical records and their contracts. Sophia had set it up so that their remuneration came directly into their bank account, which Mark appreciated. They were told of an informational staff meeting in approximately four hours once the ship left port, which would delay their evening seating, so they were temporarily given the late seating for dinner.

"I'm hungry," said Ophelia.

"Oh, just wait until you see the promenade, sweetheart. There are all kinds of things there. There's a pastry store, they have a cappuccino place where you can get custom hot chocolates, and chocolate covered jellybeans. They also have an ice cream shop and a candy store." Sophia said.

"Candy? Can we have some candy now?" Ophelia asked.

"Not until after dinner. We can pick some out, but only a sample for right now. We must find our rooms. I think maybe you should take a little nap…"

The groans from the girls were loud and unforgiving.

"If you want candy," Mark started, "You're going to have to play by the rules here. Now if you get candy before dinner, it's an exception because this is a special trip. But I don't want any guff, and I don't want you giving your mother a hard time about anything she asks you to do. There are a lot of people here and it's very difficult to keep track of everything that's going on so make it easy on us and do what you're told and stay close to us. If something should happen and you get separated, you want to find out where the information desk is and it's usually on, what is it, Sophia?"

"It's on floor three."

"It's the information desk on three." He held up three fingers. "You walk up, and you tell them you are lost, and they will contact us. They might make a loudspeaker announcement, but that's what you do if you get lost. Under no circumstances do you leave each other alone. You go together and I'd prefer that you hold hands everywhere except in the dining room. Okay?"

"Okay. Do they have a kid's area?" Carrie Ann asked.

"Of course, they do. They have a climbing wall; they have a kids' kitchen where you can do some baking and other projects. And…"

Carrie interrupted her. "Will I be stuck with the babies? Or can I go with the older kids?"

"Well honey, you're not quite old enough to go with the teenagers, so you will be with the children's group, but I'm sure they keep the babies like your sister here separate. They require different attention. But you and Ophelia will probably be together when you're there the whole time. And if you like, you can hang out with us. No problem. But once you go to the room, you must stay there for at least an hour. Okay?"

"I think it would be a good idea if we take a tour of the place too." Mark said.

"Yeah, let's do that!" said Ophelia.

They walked through the well-lit three-story promenade with stores to the right and left of them, most closed until they pulled out to sea. But several of the pizza markets, cappuccino shops, pastry and candy stores were open. There was a children's welcome center, which presented to all three girls a little backpack with the ship's logo on it. Each of the girls had a small white teddy bear inside.

They bought waters and Sophia and Mark each got a cappuccino, and then entered a candy shop that was adorned wall to wall with huge clear tubes of brightly colored candies from all over. They had vintage candies, gum, chocolate, licorice, all kinds of things. They even had the wax red lips and mustaches Mark remembered wearing as a child, and candy cigarettes that Ophelia wanted to buy, but her parents wouldn't let her.

After each girl picked out her bag, they made their

way further until they came to the ice cream shop. Mark was squinting his eyes together hoping Sophia would allow them to have a small cone, and she did.

They heard the announcement that the cabins were available, and that the luggage would be delivered during their dinner. They were due to leave port in roughly one hour 30 minutes.

They showed the girls the play center, which was two stories, with a small fenced off area for the younger children. A climbing wall was rigged with harnesses so that even the younger kids could attempt to use it, with supervision. There was an adequately staffed group of counselors there, looking young, but well-trained and very friendly. The girls were enamored with the climbing wall. One of the passenger's boys was already approaching the top and rang the bell when he got there.

They walked through the library, and Sophia showed the girls the children's section with small tables and chairs separated from the adult books. They perused up and down the rows of the big stage in the theater for evening shows, and walked through the gym with the Jacuzzis, the sauna, and then back out onto the deck to look at the swimming pool.

This ship also had a corkscrew slide and Mark knew exactly what the girls were going to be doing before dinner if they could arrange it. There was a private adult pool in the aft, where children under 12 were not admitted. There were hammocks and little tents for kids, plus large round wicker chairs suitable for the whole gang of five of them. Music was operatic. All the waiters wore black vests and bow ties and started passing out trays of champagne getting ready for the launch. The girls were brought orange juice.

At last, their drinks in hand, standing around the pool it was announced that the ship would be leaving port. With three long pulls of the horn, the ship was so loud that both girls covered their ears. They toasted to a successful trip. Mark said a little prayer, and then led them up to the 12th floor to their rooms.

Sophia had been able to upgrade since she was a former full-time employee, and they managed to have a suite at no extra cost, because this booking was so empty. It had a large balcony off the living room, which contained the red leather couch that converted to a hideabed for the girls.

Mark and Sophia's bedroom also had a sliding door to the balcony and not quite a queen-sized bed. Marc knew it would have to do.

As the ship's engines rumbled and began pushing away from the pier, they all went outside, sitting on patio chairs. Mark, holding Domenica, went to the railing, and together they watched as Napoli was left behind them, the town appearing smaller and smaller as they headed out into the deep blue waters of the Mediterranean.

The rain had stopped temporarily, but the clouds were dark gray, so they were expecting more rain this evening. But the sea was calm. White and gray shorebirds made a huge ruckus whenever the ships horns blasted.

Several vendors and tour guides and staff waved at the ship as it pulled away, Ophelia and Carrie Ann waving back. Even the baby waved.

Carrie Ann looked up at Mark. "This is fun. I can tell we are going to have a blast!"

"Absolutely, sweetheart."

As the ship moved faster, it began to feel chilly. Sophia instructed the girls to come inside and lay down for a short nap.

"We can leave the curtains open so you can be all fresh and rested for dinner tonight. Okay?"

"Mom and I have a meeting we must go to. When the time comes, we're going to take you all to the play area for a trial run."

"Okay Daddy," Ophelia said.

With the girls safely resting, Sophia took the baby in with them into their bedroom, kicked off their shoes and laid back on the pillows, watching the sites as the sun began to hang lower and lower in the sky.

"If you'll indulge me, Mrs. Beale, I'd like to go get

us some champagne or a beer or something? What would you like?"

"I don't know. Surprise me."

"Okay. Alcoholic or non-alcoholic or caffeine?" he asked her.

"You decide. I don't want to think about a single thing. I just want to sit here with her, relax for a couple of minutes and then I'll start making decisions."

"You got it."

He headed to the door but before he could open it, she called out to him.

"Hey Mark?"

"What is it?"

"I love you. And thanks for doing this. I have a feeling you and I are going to need a little bit of alone time after we get back to San Diego but thank you for putting up with all of this and for being such a good dad. I think this was a perfect way to celebrate ten years of marriage."

"It's nothing but smooth sailing from here on out. If you can last ten years sweetheart, we can last them all. And I can't think of anybody I'd rather share my life with than you and all our girls here. The best is yet to come. I promise."

CHAPTER 4

THE STAFF MEETING was held in one of the cocktail lounges large enough to hold roughly 100 people. Only the information and tour staff, medical bay/EMT services, dance and fitness instructors and special translators were there. Most of these individuals had private cabins. The bulk of the 1,500 crew members on board this ship were downstairs in the crew quarters, where they were packed four to a room, and on some of the cruise lines, had to alternate sharing beds depending on their shift.

Sophia knew it was a long grueling trip, and she had done those jobs before she earned her way up to dance instructor, but ever since she had become one of the popular staff members on the cruise, she was always given a private room, or shared with another instructor.

She didn't know most of the team present since it had been nearly a decade when she last worked this line, but several of the officers she recognized.

Mark sat next to her patiently while they waited for the tour director to show up. Old friends greeted each other, there was a little bit of smack talk about some of the officers and other staff members. There had been a generous raise given over the past year to encourage a return to work. Everyone in the industry was having trouble filling their staffing quotas. The raise was a big hit, and several noted it enthusiastically.

Sophia's salary was double what she'd received ten years prior, a pleasant surprise. It almost covered the cost of the entire vacation.

Over in the corner, stood the ship's clergy, a Catholic priest dressed in a black frock and reverse collar. He was young with sharp, angular model features. Sophia pointed him out to Mark.

"You should speak to him about redoing our vows. They usually designate one afternoon or evening and do everyone at once. But you'll have to get on the list because it fills quickly."

"Got it." Mark rose, making his way across the plum-colored thick movie theater carpet, greeting the priest with a smile and handshake.

"Sophia? Is that really you?" she heard from behind her.

Twisting in her chair she recognized Thiago, who had been a teen bus boy working on the cruise where she met Mark. He was fully grown now and had turned into an attractive young man.

"Thiago!"

"Ah, I can't believe you remember me?"

"But of course. My goodness, you grew up so handsome, look at you. And your uniform, what is your job here?"

Thiago pointed to his badge where Sophia read, *Assistant Cruise Director.*

"Very good. Wow, that didn't take long, did it?"

Thiago shook his head showing some disagreement. "Well, ten years. I guess that's not long. Sure seemed like it to me. So how is everybody in your life?"

"Well, Mark is here. He's over there talking to the priest."

"Oh, that's Father Santiago, he's very nice. You are getting married?"

"No, we've been married for 10 years, but we are going to renew our vows."

Thiago's eyes sparkled, his white teeth an attractive underscore to his dark and neatly trimmed mustache.

"I remember your romance. It was quite the talk of the staff quarters and became a problem when we got to Brazil. And all that adventure in between? My goodness. Let's hope we don't have that again!"

"No. Lightning doesn't strike twice, er, I mean a third time." She answered his puzzled expression with further explanation. "We have been on another cruise that also had issues, but not a terrorist takeover of the ship."

Her words floated across the room and, too late, Sophia realized she'd been speaking too loudly. Several of the staff members turned, frowning in her direction. She placed her hand over her mouth. "Excuse me. It was a long time ago. Much safer now," she said, stopping to check for further reaction, this time finding only two.

She brought her forehead close to Thiago, whispering, "I hope I'm not causing a problem. I shouldn't have said that Thiago. I'm going to have to apologize."

"No, don't. They've heard the stories. You remember the captain who beached his ship?"

"Oh yes, we were on that boat. One of the other passengers told us about it. Horrible."

"You were? I didn't know that."

"*After* they repaired it. But it had a forty-foot gash repair along the water line."

"Yes, well luckily they don't allow that anymore. The captains no longer have that kind of authority. He went to jail."

"I know he did. Poor man. He was just trying to save someone's life. He thought one of his American tourists was having a heart attack."

"Sophia, it was a little more than that. It was determined he had a drinking problem as well. They are extremely strict these days. So many of the old captains retired during COVID. We have a lot of fresh new former military captains, and they're excellent. I mean they're just excellent. And we have a lot more protocols for ship safety these days. The tracking and electronics are much better. It was really the Wild West when you guys went before. I'm sure other cruise lines are the same, but we've never had an incident like that since."

"Good to know. I will make sure to tell people that if it comes up."

As Mark headed back over to their seat, a rather rotund cruise director in a white uniform, also sporting epaulets and medals, came in through the back door, accompanied by a tall extremely handsome captain with a black dress uniform.

Mark stiffened. "Holy shit, it's Teseo. Teseo Dominichello, you remember him?"

"Oh, you're right. He's the captain?"

"Yes. Notice his sleeves. We're lucky. He's good."

Thiago leaned forward and extended his hand. "Sir, my name is Thiago, and I was barely legal when I last saw you. I was a bus boy in the dining room for your group. What a fun group. First time I'd met a bunch of Navy SEALs and their families. I was so impressed. Still am."

"Thank you, son."

"I haven't seen Sophia in ten years. It's nice to make your acquaintance again."

Mark continued to shake Thiago's hand.

"Did you get your ceremony arranged?" Sophia asked him.

"Tuesday night. That's when they'll do it. They'll announce it tonight at dinner."

The tour director began to address the crowd with a microphone.

"Ladies and gentlemen, if I could have your attention, please. We are pleased to welcome you to the Fantastico Nautica, our largest and most exclusive ship. Our captain is Captain Teseo Dominichello, and he has been at the helm ever since its original launch nearly one year ago."

The tall Captain waved to the crowd as they clapped for him, several standing.

The tour director continued, stepping in front of the captain. "I am Rodrigo Choppa, and I am your tour director for this cruise. I have arranged office hours from 9:00 to 10:00 in the morning, and 9:00 to 10:00 in the evening if you should need me. The ship's operator can also put you through to my state room. We are not quite full and have a very international group. Most of our passengers, as you know, come from Italy, Spain, or France. However, we do have a contingent from Denmark, we also have a large contingent from Brazil who are going to be stopping off in the States on their way back home. They have sailed with us prior and now are sailing with us for the return."

"Wow, we've got some big travelers here," whispered Mark.

"You do know that some people retire and just go from cruise to cruise to cruise. They find it's cheaper to cruise than to stay in a retirement village. It's the new thing now."

"Yeah, I'd heard that somewhere."

The microphone crackled. "I would like to have all of you who are new to this ship, please raise your hand and introduce yourselves, introduce your job, and what your nationality is or what your country of residence is please." He pointed to a young blonde woman on his right.

As the group introduced themselves, and finally came to Mark and Sophia, Mark waved to Teseo as he spoke. "My name is Mark Beale. I'm an American, and I live in California with my wife Sophia who is Italian by birth, but she is my wife, so she is an American citizen now. We met on one of these cruises, and I am fortunate enough to make the acquaintance previously of Captain Dominichello. It will guarantee that we are all in very good hands." Mark finished.

Captain Teseo shouted across the room, "And we are also in very good hands, as this gentleman here is an elite warrior."

The room was suddenly silent.

"Now, that's not a skill we're going to need on this cruise, I hope," the captain said to scores of twitters in the audience. "But I also want to put you at ease to let you know that we have one of the Navy's finest in our midst, and he is going to assist his wife as a dance instructor. We're going to see if he can walk and chew gum at the same time. He's not Italian or Brazilian, so you are going to have to forgive him if he has American feet."

The audience laughed. Mark delivered Teseo a lopsided grin. Sophia wasn't sure he was comfortable with the remarks, but he took it well.

Sophia introduced herself again in addition and explained her background in dance and what she hoped to do and mentioned that they were traveling with their three girls. "If anyone would like to earn a little bit of extra money doing babysitting, we might be interested. There may be times when the children's center is closed, but I know we have sitters on board and if you would introduce yourselves to me, I would be happy to discuss working out something. Not too much."

The meeting was short, and the later meeting, supposed to be by department, was postponed until the next morning. As they broke, Mark headed over to talk to Teseo with Sophia in tow.

Teseo addressed him with a warm smile. "Mark Beale. I never thought I would see you again."

"And I thought you were getting out?"

"Ah yes, well, you know I was in the process of a divorce last time we saw each other, and now I've fallen in love again and we are happy to celebrate the birth of our son. He's already two. So now I must work again, and this job pays well. We need to pay for his college education. She sometimes comes with me, although it's frowned upon, but she is good at the information desk and in the office, so we try to include them as much as possible, so I won't be gone for so long. Life goes on, right?"

Teseo studied Mark's eyes deeply. Sophia knew they shared something that she would ask Mark about later.

"And forgive me, I've forgotten my manners. Nice to meet you, Sophia, is it?"

"Ah! Quick recovery. You are right. I do remember that you were very quick thinking, and Mark has told me also about the other thing."

She didn't want to say what she knew from that previous mission that took Zak's eye and nearly ended in disaster.

"Oh, you mean the ambassador?" He whispered.

"Well, I wasn't going to say it. But good thinking

on your part."

Teseo agreed. "It was a lucky day for everybody. Luckily, that has never happened again either."

Mark laughed. "You mean the part about dressing him up with lipstick and a wig in a woman's dress and putting him in the freezer or the part about having to transport an important United States official back home as excess vegetables?"

Mark's grin told Sophia everything she needed to know about how he felt about Teseo's comment. It was a get even trick.

"Well yes, both. And you know, what doesn't kill you makes you stronger, right?"

"On that we agree." Mark added, "So is there anything about this particular group, anybody special who's traveling here?"

"No, I don't really recognize people even though there are several regulars I understand. But I will tell you this, and it's always this way, we are an Italian line, so we usually don't have many American tourists. I believe we have less than two dozen. We have 3,400 passengers, and yes, I think about 24 Americans. Believe it or not, we have about 50 Canadians. So, you'll find most everybody speaks English, but you're going to be hearing lots of Italian, Spanish and some French. There are the customary provincial attitudes of those passengers, and we give the Italians the toga night, where we run around with tablecloths and swing napkins over our heads. You remember, don't you?"

"Oh yes, I remember that. What an event that was."

"Here's a little secret. Your tour director, as it happens, is a former operatic star, so he will surprise you at the dinner. Italian night is Thursday, don't miss it. It's a spectacle beyond your wildest dreams."

"One of the things I like about cruising with you guys is that the food is excellent."

Teseo bowed and agreed. "Italian, of course."

"The entertainment spectacular."

"Cirque du Soleil, yes, we have excellent Russian gymnasts."

"But the ship itself is just gorgeous. I mean marble and the Murano glass, everything about this is so Italian and so beautiful—statues, waterfalls, romantic and colorful clubs, and restaurants. Even the carpet is different than other cruise ships."

"And the music of course is mostly Italian pop. Yes, that's the nice thing when you come from America and you cruise with a different country's line, you get a little bit of their culture, it's a little extra bonus for you not being Italian. I've heard it said this way."

"Your cruise director said that you are not even 90% full. Is that right?" Sophia asked.

"That is correct. We had a very large block cancel. They were following with a musical group on a special

European tour. Apparently, several of the members of the band, part of our entertainment as well, came down with COVID, so the whole thing's been postponed for a few months. Perhaps till next year. But that was a cancellation of some 300 rooms."

"Wow." Sophia was shocked.

"We try to honor repeat and loyal customers requests for refunds, especially if the band can't perform, but it's taken its toll. I'm glad we could accommodate you at the last minute. How fortunate for all of us."

"It's been a while since I've done this. We have the three girls, which we'll try to introduce you to later," Mark added.

"I would like that. Are they as beautiful as your wife?" Captain Dominichello said bowing once again.

"Absolutely. Although their mother is quite the stunner."

Teseo checked his watch. "I must get back to the bridge. Will you join me tonight at my table in the Captains Dining Room? The girls are of course invited to join you."

"They switched us to late seating tonight," said Sophia.

"Makes no difference. I don't eat much anyway, and I'm served both times. So, I'll see you at 8:30 then?"

"Absolutely. Maybe we can discuss further some of

my other questions."

"Mark, you're not going to be a worry wort, are you? With all your training and experience?"

"No, sir. But I've learned to ask lots of questions. Is there anything different that I need to pay attention to? I just want to keep my wife and children safe. Where do you have your biggest problems?"

Teseo thought about that for a minute putting his forefinger up to his lips and then spoke, "I would say we have something pop up every cruise. I have not piloted a ship where we didn't. Sometimes it's one of the waiters or the cooks or the bus boys who are fugitives. It could be that they take the job and leave port so they can escape going to jail. Occasionally we must have them arrested and take them off the ship. We have the obvious drinking issues, which is always a problem. Now, we have fentanyl. We have drugs. We have people selling drugs. And those distress me a great deal. It's very difficult to control."

"Any human trafficking?" asked Mark.

"Well, I think we did before it got so easy to just walk across your border, yes, sure. But this is a rather expensive and long way to do it. And there are more than ten days where they must be hidden and that's a long time. I don't think it's recommended or the desired way to do this. And that's a good thing. We have good cooperation with our ports of call, and I think the policing is much better than it used to be. I just think every cruise is different. There's always something that I wasn't paying attention to. And that's what I try to remember—to expect the unexpected. Because, let's face it, Mark, evil exists, right?

Sophia felt her hand close reflexively in Mark's.

Teseo added, "You know this. They never go away. The bad guys never go on vacation."

CHAPTER 5

W E PREPARED FOR a more formal dinner than we had planned. On the way, we took in the show in the Grand Theater. The snappy dance routines we thought the girls would enjoy.

The water was calm, and Mark had seen dancers do lifts and twirls and leaps when the seas were choppy, but tonight the Mediterranean was nearly like glass, the full moon sweeping its light over the still water, beaconing like a huge lighthouse. He knew just under the surface the sea was filled with unknown secrets and abundant aquatic life.

Mark had done a good deal of scuba diving both professionally and for recreation, knew it was one of the richest resources on the planet. The bed was littered with wrecked ships, odd rock croppings, giving rise to stories of lost civil civilizations buried by tons of water. Marine life was very abundant and varied.

Tonight's program was a snappy 1950s type of review, with dancers dressed in saddle shoes, full skirts, and petticoats—a takeoff on Grease or Happy Days or one of those shows. Ophelia and Carrie Ann loved it. Dominica slept in her mother's arms nearly the whole time.

Mark knew that the girls had watched their mother practice, and she had taken them to the dance studio, even attempted to teach them some ballet, so watching the dancers with their brightly colored costumes, whooping, and hollering, was extra fascinating to them. He was anxious to hear their reaction afterwards. Their eyes were relentlessly searching every movement, noise, and flash of color.

Sophia seemed to enjoy it as well.

"They're good, aren't they?" he whispered in his wife's ear.

"They usually are. They do a lot of practicing, and a lot of dancing on these cruises, it's quite a rigorous routine. But the company does pick up some of the best in the business. And it's a short commitment for the performers, a four-month contract usually, so it's something a young dancer can do when they don't have a family. It's kind of the ideal job if you're single. Great way to meet people."

Ophelia turned to her mother and put her finger in front of her lips. "Shh Mom. People are watching the show."

Mark shared a chuckle with Sophia and turned his attention back to the program.

Afterwards, as the house lights came on, they took the girls down to the stage to introduce them to some of the dancers who teased them, one of them bringing the girls up on the stage itself and pretended to polka with them very gently. Several of the other dancers chimed in, and before long, the two girls were the center of attention and loving the action, the colors, the makeup, and everything about it.

"I think we have ourselves a couple of exhibitionists here. Perhaps they have some streak of entertainer in their psyche?" he asked her.

"I think you're right. I was not attuned to this. But they really do appear to have great interest now."

"Just remember, they have to work pretty darn hard, and of course we want to impress upon them that it's not okay to just leave and join the circus when they're fifteen, right?" Mark whispered.

"Yup. I'm sure if they took their ballet shoes off and the girls could get a good look at the knuckles on their toes, their bent and sore, bruised and cut skin and bones, they'd be horrified. But they make it look easy, and fun. And that's what entertainers do. They make you think anybody could do it."

Mark was watching the lights dance in her eyes, the way she almost reverently gazed up at the stage, took in all the colors and the characters zipping past, hearing the squeals of laughter from her girls, and knew if there was a heaven, to Sophia, it would look very much like this tonight.

Later, at the captain's table, they were seated next to a couple from California who owned a winery in Sonoma County. Sophia wasn't familiar with it but stated that new wineries were popping up all the time, and it wasn't very uncommon.

The girls sat to Sophia's left and got rather fidgety with the many courses of the dinner. Once they discovered that they could order anything they wanted off the menu, the evening was saved. From then on it was all ice cream, hot dogs, and macaroni and cheese served one after the other and never refused.

Sophia leaned in and whispered to Carrie, "If you eat too much of that stuff, you're going to be sick tomorrow. And don't you want to have a nice day in the pool?"

"I eat like this all the time when I'm over at my friend's house. There we have pizza too."

The waiter overheard her comment. "Pizza? You would like pizza? We have pepperoni or we have cheese, Miss. Which would be your preference?"

"Cheese," Carrie Ann said.

"Pepperoni," barked Ophelia.

"Very well, I shall bring you a half and half. I will

be right back."

Mark spoke to the couple on his right. "I think we've just spoiled them forever. They're going to be ordering us around the kitchen learning how to do dial up takeout, it's going to be no vegetables for us or at least for them when we get home."

Everybody laughed.

Teseo raised his wine glass to Mark, and they toasted silently together across the table.

"I understand you are a Navy SEAL? Was I right in assuming that?" Mr. Brandon asked Mark.

"Yes, I am. I'm not accustomed to running around shouting about it, so feel free to keep it between us. But yes, I've been a SEAL for 12 years now. I went in right out of high school."

"Ah," Mrs. Brandon added. "How did you come to that decision?"

"Well, there was this little event called 9/11, I just felt like doing something other than watching the TV show people dying and buildings collapse in ruin. It was an easy decision for me. I wasn't enjoying college very much, and my chosen field was hopelessly boring. Accounting."

"Oh my! I can't see you being an accountant, not with what you do."

"Well, actually there are a lot of SEALs who do a lot of things. We have buddies back home that also have a winery. Frog Haven Vineyards. Have you heard of it?"

The couple shook their heads.

"You are an investor in this winery?" Mr. Brandon inquired.

"No, didn't get in on that one in time. But my other former teammate buddy runs the Lavender Farm out in Bennett Valley. He's very good at what he does, and he and his wife run an event center, a wedding center."

"Oh, I've been there. A delightful little place," Mrs. Brandon answered. "Used to be a nursery and I went there all the time."

Mark chose not to elaborate further on the history of the farm. "They work very hard at it. Sophia and I have spent many weekends up there working big parties. It's fun. Someday, perhaps we'll help them out."

"And leave San Diego?" she asked.

"I don't know. San Diego's nice, but man, there's so many beautiful places we could live in the United States. We're just biding our time. Some day."

"You won't make this a long-term career then?" Mr. Brandon asked.

"Well, I've put in 12 years, that's quite a bit for me. We'll see. It all depends on what the family wants. It's not all about me."

While Sophia headed back to the room with all three girls, Mark stayed up in the dining room hoping to have a short conversation with Teseo, who had disappeared. The American couple offered to buy him a cocktail, so they sat at the lounge, people watching and chatting. He was impatient to join Sophia and turn in early if he could.

The couple explained the development of the winery, and how they had put together investors, and had turned a relatively unprofitable piece of land into perfect soil to raise premium grapes, that they were able to sell at the highest prices.

"You don't bottle it or ferment it there on site? You just raise the grapes to sell?"

"We sell the grapes to a conglomerate," Mr. Brandon corrected. "And then we purchase bulk wine from the same conglomerate, which has some of our wine in it as well. That way we get some of the best varietals from other wineries, which is a more expensive mixture then if we just relied on our own grapes by themselves. All the new wineries are doing this now since tastes for the wine-drinking public are changing year by year."

Mark thought it sounded like a good strategy, but soon found himself becoming bored with the conversation. He remained polite, and the couple finally took their leave, allowing him to get back to the cabin.

All the girls were sleeping soundly. Sophia had moved Domenica to a small portable crib at the side of their bed and donned her favorite black silky night-gown. She was propped up in bed reading a book with her tiny nightlight.

Mark took one needy look at her, and then climbed up on the bed. "Mrs. Beale, you have good instincts. I love you in black," he said as he kissed her.

"Well hurry up and get down to your American flag boxers, then. I've got plans for those instincts."

"Your will is my command," he whispered back, and immediately disrobed.

True to his nature, Sophia had guessed his choice of boxers. He always wore the stars and stripes, or some combination of the flag colors in his boxers. It was just something he'd adopted doing when he once saw a Senior Master Chief undress on an op and never forgot it. The man was crusty as Hell, but he insisted on wearing red, white and blue, with some form of stars on his shorts, and several of the other senior officers did the same. What was good for them, was certainly good enough for Mark.

He pulled Sophia up off the bed, holding her close to him while he maneuvered the two of them to the balcony. The warm, balmy night was exciting, and as he absorbed the love in her soft brown eyes which reflected the deep yellow moon, he felt like the luckiest man alive.

She had already brought out a chilled bottle of

champagne and two flutes. He liked the way she did her advanced planning, and her recon was spot-on as well.

Smart and stubborn at the same time, what Mark really loved about her was her spontaneity and zest for life.

And the way she trembled in his arms every time he held her. She never held back showing him how she felt about him.

CHAPTER 6

T HE SHIP WAS scheduled for a sea day, so Sophia and Mark had their first ballroom dance clinic. She knew, even though he had been practicing incessantly before they left for the cruise, that he was nervous. His hands were sweaty, his arms were stiff.

As they took to the center of the floor and the music was turned on, Mark had an expression of worry, pursing his lips together and biting a side of his tongue. He had a funny habit of doing that whenever he was unsure or headed into unfamiliar territory.

He had the same reaction for speaking in front of crowds. But Sophia mused that he never was nervous going overseas, getting into a firefight, competing on the shooting range, repelling from helicopters, or doing a HALO jump at midnight in enemy territory. That was the easy stuff, he'd told her on more than one occasion.

But ballroom dancing in front of a group of nearly

seventy passengers of all ages and nationalities, skill levels, most of whom had English as a second language, was out of his comfort zone. She loved that he was so honest about giving it a good try, however. And she knew he would do his best.

He always did. It was his *only* option.

"Relax, Mark," she whispered as the music began to play. She pressed on his arms a little bit to show him how rigid his shoulders and elbows were. "Be flexible and fluid. We're going to glide, not work at it."

With one hand on her back positioned between her shoulder blades and the other clutched in hers out to the side, she whispered, "On my mark. Count of three, one Mississippi, two Mississippi, three, and we begin."

He began on the wrong foot, but she quickly skipped and matched sides with him. She had told him many times that the woman's job was to follow the man's lead always in ballroom dancing, so it was incumbent on him to make the moves to direct her. He made a lot of jokes about all the things he'd like to do to direct her, but it had nothing to do with ballroom dancing.

"I—I'm sorry."

"No problem, my love. Remember, you're right and I follow. Even if you're out of step, your cadence is wrong or the timing's wrong. You're always right." She gave him a wide grin and nodded her head as he led her into a turn while they twirled in the center of the floor.

She scanned the faces of all the onlookers and saw nothing registered in their expressions that indicated they even understood he started on the wrong foot. All except one person.

Tall and handsome, Captain Teseo Dominichello stood in the shadows just outside a secret doorway in the corner. His arms crossed his chest, his head hung to the left and his grin completely went the other way. He was in rapt attention, watching the two of them, and she saw him make eye contact each time Mark twirled her so that she was facing his direction.

On certain occasions she continued to count in a gentle purr when Mark was overly working his arms and the direction his hand gave the middle of her back. But in doing so, they stayed in step with the beat of the music. It was a beautiful waltz. They demonstrated a twirl, a turn to the right, and a graceful dip and turn to the left. At the end of the two-minute clip, they stopped, greeted each other one more time with a bow, and then released their hands to their sides.

As the audience clapped, Sophia looked up to him and smiled. "Mark, that was perfect."

But he wasn't buying any of it. She could see he was upset with himself, always obsessed with doing things 100% correctly down to the smallest detail. He was ashamed that the very first step of the dance was wrong, even though he improved. He was rigid, still nervous and hadn't yet learned to relax and just try to enjoy himself.

Sophia took the microphone and thanked everyone for their applause.

"You can see, it's a very simple step, a box step, but you can alter it by doing various turns and twirls, and you can even change it up to do double time if you're doing a jig or a faster waltz. It even begins to look like a cakewalk instead of a smooth lilting waltz. But the music and the dance steps were truly made for waltz, and if you master this, you can just about dance to any kind of music."

She demonstrated as they put on a 1940's Andrews Sisters' number, and with the syncopation in their steps, doing a move to the right, a move to the left, and then a quick step together at the end, they were essentially doing the waltz except putting emphasis on different measures in the beat.

"You can also do cha-chas and salsas with the same step. It's just a matter of whether or not you're in box formation with your partner, or you walk it up and down the line like this."

She showed a syncopated cha-cha which basically used the same steps, and by adding some hand signals, expressions, and kicks, the whole dance resembled something else, certainly not a waltz. But it was still using the same basic steps.

The crowd was ecstatic, clapping at every movement, and even when they could see Mark struggled occasionally, the laughing was all in good fun. Afterwards they received a rousing applause for the third time.

Sophia asked everyone to pair up in whatever combination they wished. There were several women who chose to dance together and even a couple of men who danced in a foursome, switching out partners occasionally. Out of the corner of her eye she saw Captain Dominichello approach the circle, take a female partner, and stand to attention like she had instructed.

"We have a celebrity in our midst today, ladies and gentlemen. Please welcome Captain Dominichello."

She motioned with both her hands in his direction, and he took a bow, grinning.

From past dance classes, Sophia knew that all the ladies in the room, especially the single ones, were going to be cutting in on Captain Dominichello, which was as it should be. The captain was always Prince Charming at the Cinderella ball.

Mark observed as she walked around the circle and helped everybody position their arms properly. When she came to Captain Dominichello, his partner was a young buxom woman. She decided to address this head-on.

"Now in this instance, Captain, you have to judge what's a safe space for *her*, not what you might desire," she said not making eye contact. "There are some women that are girthy, and you need to leave room for that, other women who are well-endowed unlike me."

The woman spoke up quickly.

"Oh, please Sophia. It's no problem for me. He can squeeze me as tight as he wants to," said in an attractive southern drawl.

"Ah, one of our two dozen Americans then, is that correct?"

"Yes ma'am, I'm Noreen, and I am from Georgia, yes ma'am."

Captain Dominichello firmly splayed his fingers against her back and did not force her to come closer to him, however, Noreen took the opportunity to sneak in a step closer and made sure her front side happened to brush up against his, which caused a slight ripple amongst the others in the class.

After Sophia completed correcting all the body positions, adjusting fingers and the way the male partner held the female partner, she demonstrated with Mark, showing how he held his hand out like a cup and how she placed her two middle fingers in the center of that cup and used it as a gauge. In this way, they demonstrated how she could twirl and not lose her bearing, be aware of how close or far away her partner was.

"Sometimes it gets quite busy. You're avoiding other couples, and it's very helpful that you don't have to look at his hand to know exactly where you are. And remember ladies, the man is *always* right." Before she returned to Mark, she noted that Captain Dominichello was beaming. It concerned her a little, but she was used to Italian men being rather loose and forward, and though she was Italian by birth, she was now an American, and American women were always fair game for Italian men.

"Okay, ladies and gentlemen, we're going to try to twirl while stepping in time to the music. So, we are going to count one two three four, one two three four, repeatedly. You are to make your turn in the count of four."

A couple of the elderly couples who were normally used to using canes or walkers, struggled a bit with this so Sophia helped them with the modification and instead of twirling, they could move gently and gracefully from side to side, "One two three four to the right. One two three four to the left."

After a few more demonstrations she asked Mark to join her in the center again and they demonstrated the box step of the waltz, about ten times before she cut the music.

"Now what I'm going to do is dance with all the

opposing partners, males or females, whichever you have, and I'm going to have Mark dance with the women partners or opposing partners man or woman. Now remember Mark is the person who is always right. And ladies your job is to do whatever he does. Now if he goes one two three, one two three four, that's what you do. If he goes one two and stops and tries to do it all over again you match his steps. On the dance floor, if the woman matches what the man does nobody is ever going to notice whether he is doing the steps correctly or if he keeps time with the music. If you two are in sync, the dance looks good. Are we clear about that?"

The group was excited to get moving, and Sophia played a long piece that repeated itself. She followed around and danced with all 30 men in the audience. She was surprised, that many of them were quite good dancers and had good balance on their feet. Most were even more relaxed than Mark was.

Mark struggled a bit with the women, having difficulty taking charge. So, Sophia decided to stop the music and make it a teaching moment.

"I want to ask you ladies, what did you learn dancing with Mark?"

"He's a good dancer," somebody said.

"Thank you" Mark replied.

"I found it hard to follow him. But I think we got in

sync," someone else nodded, and Mark acknowledged it. Agreeing.

"Anything else?"

"Actually, it really didn't matter whether he stayed with the music or whether he used his right or his left foot or gave me the instruction to turn, I just tried to match his every movement but on the reverse side. It actually was quite easy."

Delighted with the answer, Sophia clapped for the student.

"Bingo, we have a winner. That's the right answer. Dancing is easy. When you stress about it, when you get tense, when you worry about how you look, you don't dance well. You need to relax and just dance as if you know how and remember that the more you dance the better you get."

Sophia got another ovation.

"I remember hearing an interview with Ginger Rogers and Fred Astaire. She was his all-time favorite partner, and the comment was made that Fred Astaire and Ginger Rogers always made it look so easy. Somebody asked her, 'How did that happen? Did you just spend every waking moment practicing?'"

Several people knew the story and started to nod.

"Fred Astaire said, 'It's actually very easy for me. Because the man is always right. What she must do is follow my lead. The man never makes a mistake, right

Ginger?' He said to her."

"The questioner then asked Ginger the same question. Her answer was this, 'Sure, it's very easy to just follow Fred's steps, except I get to do it in high heels and backwards.'"

"But even Ginger Rogers made it look easy, and it will be easy the more you do it. So have fun, practice all you can. There are numerous little clubs and bistros all over the ship. You can even practice by the pool if you want in your bathing suit. There's no right or wrong way to master your ballroom dancing skills. You can get together with three or four or five couples and practice all your dance steps, even choreograph a few things where you switch partners, all that is simply a function of enjoying what you're doing."

Sophia had finished the hour lesson with moving about the dance floor and demonstrating some individual turns that she had perfected, certain movements that sent her off in the distance and then they reconnected in the middle of the floor later, indicating that if they advanced, they would be learning some of these steps as well.

"I hope you have enjoyed our lesson today; it was a pleasure. Mark and I had a great time. And I'm going to leave the music running for another half hour, so you can practice but this is the end for today. And thank you."

Again, the audience gave both she and Mark hearty applause.

One of the older ladies grabbed Mark's arm and sashayed with him across the dance floor, obviously not listening to anything Sophia had said, because she was guiding Mark, leading him instead of vice versa. Sophia found it funny and enjoyed watching the battle of the sexes in front of her.

From behind her, she heard a deep voice. "May I have this dance please Instructor Beale?"

She didn't have to turn around to know it was the gravelly voice of handsome Captain Dominichello. She curtsied and said, "With pleasure."

Captain Dominichello was quite good at ballroom dancing, and probably had taken lessons so that he could play his part well.

"You're a good dancer, captain."

"My mother forced me to take ballroom dance lessons when I was in early school. It was not the sort of masculine activity I liked, but I'm grateful to her now that she insisted."

Sophia recognized the scent of his cologne, guessed it was Italian, a little on the flowery side, with a bit of spice mixed in. Italian men seemed to enjoy using citrus, bergamot, and honeysuckle, along with a healthy dose of all-spice mixture. On a woman, the scent would be delicious. On a man, it was absolutely devastating. She was going to have to buy some for Mark.

"May I ask you a question?"

"Absolutely. Fire away."

"What is that scent?"

"Ah, it's a private mixture blended for me. I buy it on the Island of Capri. I can send you a bottle if you like. I don't have any extras with me, but I can have a bottle sent to you if you like."

"Oh, just the name, you don't have to buy me a bottle I'm sure it's expensive."

"But so well worth it. I shall smile every time I think of it. The lovely Sophia buys it for her husband. I think that's romantic, don't you?"

"It is." She toyed with the idea of laying some ground rules and decided it was time to do so. "I have to tell you, that Mark and I are happily married. I am very happy to be dancing with you, but I don't want you to misunderstand me."

"But nothing like that is intended, Sophia. I just enjoy the company of beautiful women, intelligent, cultured, beautiful women. I guess I haven't been fully domesticated."

"Well, I think you probably are a smart gentleman as well, and you wouldn't do anything that would jeopardize my comfort on this cruise. Mark is good at a lot of amazing things. He probably would've had a hard time if he lived during Queen Victoria's time and was a man at court. I think he would find it too restrictive, and not at all fun. But I give him kudos for always trying, and always willing to support me. He gives me a long leash."

"Indeed, he does," the captain whispered.

"And that's because he knows he can trust me."

CHAPTER 7

MARK WAS HEADED with Ophelia and Carrie Ann to the pool, expecting to ride with them down the corkscrew-tunneled tube splashing into the deep end. They ran smack dab into the second seating crowd for lunch, coming in the opposite direction, and for a moment he lost sight of the girls ahead of him. But as they waited for the elevator, he caught up to them and they took it up to the 12th floor where the pool deck was.

Ophelia had brought her bag stuffed with a book, her teddy bear, and some of her candy. They found three chaises next to each other, and then located a big wicker daybed with a canvas cover to block the sun. They laid out their towels and stashed their bags, heading for the ladder leading up to the tubes.

Mark was impressed with the speed of the slide, and how fast they dropped. The girls, who followed behind him one at a time, were visibly shaken when they got to the bottom. He caught them mid-air as they came shooting out about ten feet from the spout.

"Should we do it again?" he posed.

Ophelia immediately shook her head. "I don't think so. Unless I ride with you? Like sit on your lap?"

"Sure." He looked over at Carrie Ann. "Kiddo, are you okay?"

"That was really fast Daddy, but I want to do it again. I'm not scared."

"Okay then let's hop on up there."

The second time down was much better, and although Ophelia was screaming the whole way, it was nothing but good fun. They took turns riding with him for the next half hour, and finally Ophelia admitted that she was tired.

They skipped the seated lunch, so Mark ordered hot dogs and sodas, and they sat in the little tented chaise, almost like a camping experience in their own backyard. The food tasted excellent, the girls ate their chips and hot dogs and asked for more.

Mark wanted to sample some of Ophelia's candy. "Can I have something from your bag?"

"Sure Daddy." She pulled the pink plastic bag out of her beach carryall and handed it to him.

Without looking too closely Mark dug in, swarming around and then looking to see if he could find anything made of chocolate. But his eyes landed on a cellophane bag holding what appeared to be a tiny bag of colored cereal loops. He knew from the work that they'd been doing down in Mexico and other places, that this was not candy, not cereal, but drugs. His daughter had drugs in her candy bag!

"Ophelia? Where did you get this?" He held up the bag.

"There were some kids running down the hallway last night, and one of them dropped it. I asked him if he wanted it back and he didn't hear me. So, I just kept it."

"Have you taken any of these?"

"No."

"Well, these are not cereal or candies these are very harmful. Who were the kids that you saw with these bags, and did you see if they had any more?"

Ophelia got pensive and then added, "The boy who dropped it has red hair. But they didn't speak English and I don't know where they are."

"How many of them were there?"

"Five or six of them—all boys. But the one who dropped it, he had really curly red hair."

"So would you recognize him if you saw him again?"

"I think so. But I don't want to get him in trouble. What if it wasn't his? What if I made a mistake?"

"Did you steal it?"

"No Daddy, I wouldn't do that."

Carrie Ann inserted herself into the conversation. "I saw what happened, and Ophelia's right, they dropped it. I don't remember the red-haired boy, but I've seen the boys around. They hang out in the video rooms, and they were at the teen dance, I think. We walked past it last night if you remember."

"Yes, I remember that. They go to the teen parties, they're not young men but teenagers?"

"They look like high school to me. I don't know. But I'll tell you if I see them again." Carrie Ann was satisfied, but Mark knew he had to alert the medical director, as well as Teseo about this new development. And he needed to find Sophia to let her know as well.

"Carrie Ann, do you have anything like this in your bag?"

She looked down at her lap. "I finished mine."

Mark's stomach lurched. "But you didn't eat anything like this did you?"

"No, I don't like those anyway."

"Just so you know, these are not candy. You wouldn't like them. And they can kill you. And if those boys are carrying this on the ship, there are kids who are in danger here. We have to do something about it."

Ophelia began to cry.

Mark grabbed her and gave her a hug, smoothing her hair and whispering to the top of her head. "It's okay sweetheart. You didn't do anything wrong. I'm just glad I found this. God, I would not forgive myself if something like this happened to you. This is very, very dangerous."

"I'm scared. Do you think those boys would hurt me if they found out I told on them?"

Mark thought about it and decided to lie. "Oh no, they aren't going to know it was you and your sister. They don't even know that you picked it up. I wouldn't worry about it. But if we don't tell somebody, if someone else picks it up and eats it, could be very bad. And we're going to stop that from happening."

"MARK, I'M GLAD you brought this to my attention," said Teseo. "We've received warnings but you're the first person who found these."

"Just a lucky break she didn't ingest any of these."

"Indeed. I'll call the office. We'll have to find these kids. It's good that your girls will be able to recognize them. The fact that they're not English speakers doesn't do us much good, but the red hair. That will help us out."

"Do you think these kids are selling this stuff or using it? Mark asked.

"Doesn't matter, Mark. It's illegal as hell. And depending on what port of call we come into, different countries have a very different way of handling this.

Like, you don't want to have any kind of drugs on you in Morocco, even though they openly smoke hashish. But any kind of pills or other drugs? It can be a prison sentence for kids who are way underage. They have a big problem with that. I'm going to have to find their parents, and figure out what circle they're traveling in. But we're going to isolate them and get them off the ship."

"Thank you. Sorry about this, but just thought you should know."

"Oh absolutely. This is just like what I told you the other night. We never used to have things like this happen and now, it's hard to separate the good people from the bad people, if you know what I mean. The kids sometimes on these cruises are left to run around on their own in packs and they do get into trouble. On one of the ships one of my captains caught them setting fire to one of the lifeboats on deck seven. I can't imagine kids who would think it's okay to be that destructive or violent. Melted the whole thing, ruining it. And it was a black mark against the company."

"Well, you let me know if we need to do anything else."

They were due to come to port that evening, docking at a private cruise ship island off the coast of Italy, and the next day there were several shore excursions people had signed up for. Sophia and Mark hadn't decided to do that and were going to rent a car or just stay at the beach all day. They weren't interested in taking a tour of anything.

As the sun was setting, he headed back towards his cabin. Behind him he heard laughter, and spotted a group of teens laughing, kicking a beer bottle around the deck as if playing soccer, until it finally broke and then the kids chucked it overboard.

"Hey! You guys stop that," Mark shouted. "That's glass, people walk around here barefoot all the time. Are you idiots?"

Two of the boys mounted a very lackluster "I'm sorry," chorus. They were not interested in receiving any of Mark's correction. He halfway expected to see the red-haired boy in the middle of them. They spoke English, but their native tongue was Italian.

The boys drifted off around the corner while Mark was looking for a waiter to get something to clean up the glass.

Dinner was seated, and Mark was starved. They were sharing a table with four other people, two couples. Since it was the habit of the cruise line to place people at tables who shared a common language, he thought that he'd probably be seated with Americans.

As Mark's family sat down, the couple from California joined them, as well as another couple from New York. Introductions were made and Mr. Brandon, made a pitch to Mark about investing in his winery.

"You know, I've been thinking about what you said about the wineries, the ones your friends have?"

"Frog Haven you mean?"

"Yes. You know, we do investment pools with our winery where you can buy a share, and then you get a percentage of the vintage for the year. We sell off the others to our distributors, and you get a share of the profits in that. It's actually a very nice arrangement, because you get good quality wine for a decent price, and you're encouraged to share the wine with other people because it can make you additional money as well if they also buy in. I'm not sure what kind of discretionary funds you have, but we even take small denominations, as investors. You should think about that," Brandon said.

Mark wasn't interested in the slightest, keeping what little cash they had left over for the possible move to a larger house someday soon, and for the girls' education. But he thanked the gentleman. The missus was adorned with expensive jewelry, large diamond rings and gold dangle bracelets banded several inches up from her wrist toward her elbow. She was heavyset, but with her rosy complexion and extra makeup, was far more attractive than he had noticed her the night before.

The dinner came as usual, in seven courses and the

girls got fidgety. Mark and Sophia dismissed them-selves early, so the rest of the group could enjoy their meal. Dominica was fussy and running a small fever. While Sophia put her to bed, Mark read a story to Carrie Ann and Ophelia, until they both fell asleep.

"Are they all done?" Sophia whispered.

"Yes ma'am."

"What is Captain Dominichello going to do about this? Have you heard anything more?"

"No. But I was thinking of walking around and see-ing if I could maybe locate these kids on my own. I studied the dining hall tonight to see if I could find anybody but didn't see anyone that matched their description."

"Oh, so you did that too huh? So did I."

"You know it's going to fester until we find them. I'm just surprised that they're so blatant about bringing drugs onboard. And where the hell are their parents? I didn't realize this type of thing could even happen on a ship like this. I mean I think they checked the bags for weapons and things. But I'm not sure how they got these drugs on board."

"Well maybe it was a staff person who brought it on board, or maybe they brought it on their person instead of in the luggage. You know kids who want to do drugs, they'll find it anywhere. And if they have money, and their parents are off doing whatever else they're doing, they'll get in trouble. I feel sorry for them though. Very dangerous."

"You know I think I will walk around and see if I can find a couple of the hangouts, and just look into it a bit. You okay with that?"

"Absolutely. You go do that. I'm going to turn in early. I know tomorrow we're going to have a busy day, so I'll just get the rest. Don't be late though. No gambling Mark. And stay away from the Brandons."

"No way am I going to involve them."

Mark changed his clothes, donning a pair of khakis, flip-flops, and a long-sleeved T-shirt. He wore a baseball cap and his aviators, even though it was nearly dark, but he thought it would make a good disguise in case he was spotted. He didn't want to trigger anybody's attention.

He walked down the promenade, poking his head into the different stores, especially the candy store and a couple of the shops that catered to people buying electronic devices, movies, and music.

Sounds of the ship slowing down, were followed by the motors complete shut off. One quick glance outside and he determined that they were already in port, tied up for the next day's excursions.

Several of the bars were going to close early, and there was a two-story brightly colored dance and party room for teens, that had a billiard table, mirrored dance floor, and brightly painted murals on the walls. There were roughly 20 kids in there, boys and girls, but again, Mark didn't see any teenagers who looked like they were from the group he saw, or the boys Ophelia saw.

He turned a corner and almost ran into a freckle-faced kid with bright red hair who was about a foot shorter than he was. There was no question in Mark's mind that this was the kid who dropped the drugs.

"Hey, I want to talk to you."

The boy with several others behind him, pushed Mark so hard that he fell on his rear, while they took off running, eventually breaking through double doors to the outside balcony. Mark scrambled to get back on his feet and followed the series of noises he heard at the end of the hallway, hearing a door open, music blaring and then stopping when the door slammed shut. They had run down the outside balcony and returned to the interior of the ship, somewhere near the theater. He ran after them hoping to catch glimpse of exactly where they wound up. But he had no luck. There were no teens to be found anywhere in this vicinity.

He walked back out through the double doors, scanning both directions of the balcony, traveling down the line of bright orange rescue boats tethered to the sides on this floor. He even peered inside several of the windows to see if the kids might be hiding inside the boats. But he found nothing.

One by one, he examined underneath the boats inside and down toward the railing which faced the sea, not the port side. He was leaning over the balcony after hearing sounds of voices trying to get a glimpse, when suddenly someone came up behind him and pushed him over the edge into the water.

He took a hard fall in the water, not expecting to be tossed, and shouted for help. He wasn't worried about being able to tread water, but he was concerned with the equipment on the ship, and the temperature of the water at nighttime. A large doorway was slid open as several of the crew who were washing windows on the lower two decks, noticed his fall and quickly came to his aid, tossing him a lifebuoy, and dragging him up into the hull of the ship.

"What happened?" Asked an older gentleman in a white painter's overalls. He spoke broken English, with a heavy Russian accent.

"Somebody pushed me over the railing. I think some kids did it."

"Kids?" The man asked.

"I was following some. Perhaps you know, the captain has found drugs on board ship. I'm not sure the word has got out yet, but there are some kids apparently who have drugs."

"Here, you take this, and you should get back to

your cabin, but are you okay? Do you want to be seen by the doctor?"

He handed him a warm blanket that had just come out of the dryer. It felt heavenly.

"Is your ship's physician here right now?" Mark asked.

"He is. Why don't you come this way." The man and two of his helpers accompanied Mark as two others closed the door and wiped up the excess water from Mark's re-entry. He knew that he was going to have to report this as well to Captain Dominichello. He remembered the comment one of his teammates had made before he left, and he remembered vowing that there was going to be no way he'd be bobbing in the water. Well cross that one off the bucket list he thought.

The ship's doctor and medic approached him and did a cursory check of his vitals.

"Did you hit the side of the ship on the way down, does anything feel bruised or cut?"

"No. I'm fine. Really."

"You know the sides of these ships are loaded with chains and hooks and all kinds of things I have seen some awful cuts and we have crew that fall all the time. When you get back to your cabin and you notice something please let us know."

The doctor looked up at the overalled gentleman

who helped Mark. "Damien? You will make an incident report of this?"

Damien nodded agreement. "Si si, I will make sure it's done within the hour."

"You bring it to me, and I'm going to take it to Teseo."

"Okay fine Doctor."

Damien left the group and Mark asked if he could bring the blanket with him to his cabin.

"Oh sure. Give it to your porter tonight or tomorrow when you're done. Now let me ask you this, did you see whoever pushed you?" The doctor asked.

"I did not. I didn't hear a thing. I was chasing the boys, so perhaps it was somebody from their group, there were four of them. But no, I didn't see or hear anybody."

"Well, son, you're very lucky. You go back, I'll make sure Captain Dominichello knows about this, and here," the doctor handed him an injury form in triplicate. "I want you to fill this out and have it ready for the captain. Can you do that?"

"I will. What about these kids?" Mark asked.

"Let's get the incident registered first, and then we'll see what the captain wants to do about searching the ship for them. It sounds like we have a problem. In my experience, it's never a good idea to sleep on a problem. There's going to be a few of us working all night long to try to figure this out. Thank you for bringing it to our attention. And I am so sorry this occurred."

CHAPTER 8

S OPHIA HEARD MARK'S voice outside the cabin door, engaging in heated conversation with their cabin steward. She was sitting in bed, exhausted from the last hour and a half when Domenica woke up screaming, with a higher fever than she'd had earlier in the day, her gargantuan diaper filled to overflowing all over the cradle and bedsheets, including her blanket. After a full change and bath, she was safely asleep again, but not before she woke up her two older sisters. As soon as Domenica dozed off Sophia jumped in the shower and changed her nightie as well.

Mark was back later than he told her he would be.

The cabin door opened. Sophia was shocked to find her husband standing in front of her with a blanket draped around him, a dripping wet blanket. She examined the growing puddle at his feet. He had an unpleasant expression on his face.

"Whatever the hell—"

Mark interrupted her. "Let's just say it's been a bad evening." He strained to step out of his khaki pants, which stubbornly clung to him. He was barefoot. Next, he slipped off his shirt, and attempted to take off his baseball cap and glasses, but then swore.

"Goddammit, I left them."

"You left them? What do you mean?"

"It's a long story, but let me get clean and dry first, okay?"

Naked, he carefully opened the cabin door and tossed the blanket into the hallway where it was retrieved by their steward. After further conversation, Mark using the door as a privacy shield, she realized that her husband had arranged for their steward to stand by to take the blanket away.

"Did you get thrown in the pool Mark?"

"No, I got thrown in the sea." He gave her that blank stare, waiting for her to get the significance of what he just told her. "Somebody threw me overboard."

At first, she'd thought it was a joke, but then realized he wasn't kidding. "Overboard? As in over the railing? Where?"

"Deck 12, at least that's where I started from. I wound up coming in through one of the cargo bays down at level one. I had some help getting out."

"Did you get in a fight?"

Exasperated, he threw his hands down at his naked sides, looking every bit the drowned rat. Whispering, "Sophia, for Christ's sakes. No, I didn't get in a fight. I don't do that anymore. Somebody just threw me overboard."

"But why? What did you do?"

"You think because I got thrown overboard that I must have done something to cause this? Are you fucking kidding me?"

His voice had carried, and the timbre was urgent, soaring into higher decibels, which caused Carrie Ann to stir.

"Please, don't wake the kids." She whispered, adding a glare.

Mark shrugged his shoulders, kicked his khakis and shirt into the bathroom, and pulled the shower door closed behind him.

Sophia carefully got up, confronting him as he turned on the water. "So where are your Aviators and your Team 3 cap? I thought you were going incognito tonight?"

"Apparently it didn't work, Sophia. Somebody must have seen through the disguise."

"I just don't understand this, I mean people have to have a reason to throw someone overboard—"

"Well, maybe it has to do with the drugs I discovered, or I don't know maybe somebody just got drunk and felt like it," Mark sputtered through the water.

"Where are your flip-flops then? You walked all the way down the hallway and through the promenade dressed like that? In a wet blanket? Barefoot?"

"Last I saw, my flip-flops were headed to North Africa in the current. Thank God we had already docked, or who knows, you might still be looking for your husband."

"Well, I can see you're in no mood—"

"You think?" Mark again stared at her, shampoo running down his forehead into his eyes. He brushed the soap clear and spat.

Something about the whole situation was becoming comical, but Sophia didn't dare show it. She'd let him have the next say.

"I'm just as surprised as you are. And no, I didn't see who did it. I wish the hell I did, but I have some ideas. Now if you don't mind, I'd like to take my shower and get myself right, and if you could bring me my pajama bottoms, I promise when I get dry and get clean, I will come out and sit and talk to you in the bedroom okay?"

"Fair enough."

She searched through the small dresser next to Mark's side of the bed and retrieved his red, white, and blue drawstring cotton pajama bottoms. She hesitated but decided not to bring him his T-shirt. That was for her own benefit. Perhaps she would be able to find some way to sweeten him up a bit. But he was extremely angry, and probably felt ridiculous.

She folded the pajama bottoms and left them on the toilet seat. She also added an extra towel from the bedroom and retrieved his wet clothes after wringing them in the sink.

Tiptoeing through the living room, she exited the sliding glass door from their room and placed his khakis and T-shirt over the railing. They weren't supposed to do this, but she thought under the circumstances she might be forgiven.

Sounds of the little village where they would be spending some time tomorrow were drifting across the dark water on the wings of a gentle breeze. She heard music, drums, and laughter. All along the Mediterranean coast of Italy and France, it was a continual party, starting at the eastern coast of Italy, around the boot and winding up on the coast of Spain at Mallorca. Things changed drastically once the landscape turned to North Africa. But the whole Mediterranean coast was filled with yachts and jetsetters staying in all the countries in between, socializing, gambling, and living the life of the rich and famous. It was the Europeans' playground par excellence.

The door opened behind her and Mark, smelling wonderful, stepped out onto the balcony, placing his towel over the railing, and then sitting next to her on the plastic deck chair.

"At last. I've never had this happen to me before. If some of the team guys were on board, I'd accuse them. But no way this was a prank. I think it was those damn kids."

"So, you found them?"

"Yup. Ran right into the carrot top. And he's one ugly little kid. Mean too. He took off as soon as we connected, and I tried to keep up, but the deck was wet, and there were people out there, a lot of chairs and kids and stuff to avoid. I didn't quite make it. He disappeared into the interior. I searched the theater and several other places, including a couple of hangouts, but no luck. I decided to wait outside and considered that maybe he'd show his face again. He was with a group of several other kids. They're about 13, 15, something like that."

"Do you think one of his buddies came to get him or went after you to defend him?"

"I have no idea. I wouldn't have thought that a kid could do that to me because I hung on. But I twisted around to see if I could make heads or tails of who was there, and I didn't see a thing. No shouts, no language, no nothing just picked me up by the shins, and tossed me right over like yesterday's meal. Fucking idiot. I'm just lucky I didn't scrape my back or arms or legs on some of those God-awful hooks that are embedded in the hull. You know, the ones they use for tying things off and hoisting?"

"Yeah, it's a regular workstation there by the cargo door. On both sides. They winch a lot of things through there, depending on the port they're at. You were just lucky somebody saw you."

"Well, the ship had stopped. I heard the engines stop before I got tossed. It was still moving very slightly until it hit the edge. That kind of threw off my balance, and then boom I was gone."

"Lucky thing they didn't get you on the port side, that might have proved to be fatal."

"You can say that again. Ouch. Well, I wasn't on that side, so I guess if I had, it would be a different story, wouldn't it?"

"Did you report this to Teseo?"

"No, I've got a goddamn form I have to fill out and submit to him. He said they were going to be doing an investigation all night long to see if they could locate the kids. They won't get away with it."

"You said he? One of the engineers or crew hands?"

"Yes. A Russian guy helps in the engine room—he's an engineer. I've got the paperwork; I'll fill it out and then have our steward take it up to the bridge."

Sophia was concerned at the obvious attack on her husband. She was grateful that he wasn't with the girls, and she was also grateful that she wasn't the one targeted.

The cruise, only being two days now, was already turning into quite an adventure, on the negative side.

"So how was your evening?" Mark asked, finally.

"You don't want to know. Domenica woke up with a fever, screaming her head off, wet all the way through every layer she had, almost soaking the mattress. I had to rip everything off and dump it in the hallway while Corky gave us some cleaning wipes and two extra sets of linens for her crib. I gave her a small bath in our bathroom, and she was happy, after that her temperature reduced slightly, and I gave her cough syrup so she could sleep and reduce the fever. She went right to bed. Out like a light. But then Carrie Ann and Ophelia, they were moaning, awake and rather upset with their little sister. I let them watch about a half an hour TV, and then Ophelia had already fallen asleep, Carrie Ann had to be convinced, but they went down. No big deal. I do it all the time at home, but we have a larger house."

"Yep, much easier in a small place to keep everybody controlled. I guess I should thank our lucky stars for such a tiny house."

"Mark, it'll change. You'll see. Maybe this is a signal that we should be searching our other options. I have lots of help with the wives, but three kids when you're gone for weeks at a time, I'm not happy with that. But we'll talk about it when we get home. Right now, I'm exhausted and glad to have you back. I need to get some sleep."

"Well, that dashes the second plan I had for this evening," he said.

Sophia smiled. "Hold on there, sailor, not entirely. I can be convinced. Don't give up on me yet."

Mark leaned over and planted a deep kiss on her lips. She still tasted the salt water from the sea, and scent of shampoo, which still overpowered the nice cologne she'd bought him today.

Mark kissed her again. "I've only just begun, sweetheart."

CHAPTER 9

MARK GRABBED SOME fruit and a bagel and cream cheese, packed up some bananas and apples and several yogurts for the girls, who weren't hungry yet. He gathered his little brood together and they were one of the first groups to line up going through the crew bypass of the metal detector, and down the gangway to the pier.

"One of the things you got to remember on these ships is you want to be one of the first ones off the ship," Sophia said.

"Why is that?"

"The vendors and hucksters aren't quite ready yet, still drinking their coffee and chewing the fat with their colleagues. They get kind of geared up after a few minutes and the bulk of the population exits. That's when it's like threading a gauntlet. They're going to leave us alone. Besides, we're wearing our badges and they don't treat the staff the same as they do the guests."

One of the perks of being a staff member was that they got to use the staff exit, which was much faster than waiting in the long lines for the tourists to line up and be called by grouping. They were staged all over the boat. A line of five buses waited for the offloading passengers.

"You've been on this tour before?" Mark asked.

"No this is a new island for them. But I'd rather go to a real place, not a company-owned island if I was doing a tour. This is a beach party today in the Mediterranean, but not a shopping tour especially. But they will take them all over the mountain, which is an extinct volcano. It's like the Canaries here. Except it's a little warmer even."

"So, you *have* been here."

"No, I read about it. I had no interest in doing any of the bus groups. Besides I think the girls would get carsick."

Mark was carrying Domenica in the baby pack on his front side, her legs bouncing, as she was pointing and giggling and having a good time looking at all the colors of the island. Mark discovered she liked music as well. The older girls encouraged her and had taught her to dance, which was cute as hell.

"Well Domenica's liking it, that's a good thing. She doesn't feel warm to me now."

"I think she just had to sweat it off. When she's happy, you know she's not sick."

Mark used his long strides to get past the small contingent of greeters and tour guides trying to sell tickets to unfilled buses. He waved them off carefully and then turned around, realizing that he had forgotten the rest of his family, who were hanging back looking at embroidered tablecloths, something Sophia had been looking to purchase on this trip. Mark waved to her, and she took the girls by their hands, and all three of them ran to his side.

"Did you get a car?"

"I did even better. I got a driver."

Sophia put her hand up to her forehead to block the sun. "You did not do that. Really?"

"I did."

"In light of everything that's been going on, and you certainly don't know this fellow. I mean, is this wise?" Sophia asked him.

"I think so. Besides, my fanny pack has more than just my wallet in there. I dare the son of a bitch who tries to interfere with our little tour group."

"But Italy's pretty strict on gun control, Mark."

"Listen, we do this for a living, right? I know what I can get away with and what I can't. I have a special badge. You, on the other hand if you carry one, you'll get in trouble. The only difference between you and I sweetheart, love of my life, mother of my girls—"

He kissed her gently.

"Only difference is, I don't care what the fuck they do to me. And you do."

"Somebody has to take care of the kids."

Pierre, their driver, had a handlebar mustache, wore white pants and a striped navy and white long sleeve T-shirt, and a beret. Mark was sickened with his attire when he announced himself and asked him rather forcefully if he could please remove his beret.

First order of business was replacing the hat that Mark lost in the water. This involved the girls, and they had a delightful time showing him tie dye reggae hats with dreadlocks sprouting from the brim, or hats with naked women on them, or dumb sayings like 'life is just a beach'. Finally, with Sophia's help, they chose a navy-blue hat with an anchor on the front, and that was damn close to something he would have bought for himself.

Next, he had to get a new pair of Aviators but when he discovered the prices, chose a cheap pair instead. He could get one when they had one of the sales on board ship later and wasn't going to pay two hundred dollars plus for a knockoff.

They had burned up the first forty-five minutes of Pierre's time, so Mark asked him if he could take them to a nice, secluded beach area where they could just lay out their towels and wade in the water if it wasn't too choppy.

"Oui, oui. There are many such places. Do you want to snorkel?"

Mark almost didn't answer him because it suddenly occurred to him that being dressed as a Frenchman, with a name like Pierre but working in Italy, was such a mismatch, he wondered why he didn't notice it before. He had to ask him.

"No snorkel today. But say, Pierre, I assume you're French?"

"Mais oui. I live here now, my wife is an Italian citizen, so we live here close to her family."

"Oh, I see. That completely explains it. You live on the island?"

"No, it is not that type of an island, resources are very limited. I live in Capri, you've heard of it, the place for lovers?"

"Oh yes we've both been there," Sophia said. "Lovely place. I'd like to do that too but I'm not sure how much time we're going to have."

"I don't believe your ship has more than three or four hours there. But I could meet you at port and drive you up over the mountain and back again. But that's about it. No shopping, just a sight-seeing trip and it's long and windy."

"Yes, I know. I think you'll have to save it for another time. But if we manage to get a sitter, maybe Mark and I will do that." She wiggled her eyebrows at her husband who matched the expression.

"Well then, my dear, take my card. You can call me from your cell phone tonight and let me know if it would work out. I'm sure they have someone who could babysit for a few hours for you. I know lots of cute little restaurants and bars that you would just love. Things have changed quite a bit since COVID. We have new people here. We have a lot of the old places shut down and rebuilt. And we had several Mediterranean storms about two years ago that damaged a lot of the coastline. But all the favorite places are still there, and of course the scenery, the drive, is beautiful."

"Absolutely. The most beautiful scenery I've ever seen in my life," said Sophia.

She saw that Mark had made a note of it and before she could take Pierre's card, he grabbed it from his fingers and placed it in his pocket.

"We'll see if we can do something about that later on. Thanks Pierre. Now, where are we going to?"

"On the other side, on the shoreside of the island, you can look across the inlet and see the mainland of Italy. It's a most beautiful location, and they have a resort there that caters to American tourists and other celebrities, and they've imported a sand beach. The best beaches of course are on this side, but you have no view."

Mark pointed to the bright blue sky and the turquoise horizon of the Mediterranean. "I'd say that's a pretty damn good view, wouldn't you?"

"Indeed. But if you want that view, you can go to Florida. You can go to Brazil, you can go to a beach in Southern California, or New Jersey. This beach has beautiful sugar white sand just like what you Americans have in Florida, and you can see all the terracotta villages that are stair stepped on the mainland. You can see the vineyards in this very famous agricultural region."

As promised, the views were outstanding, and several times Sophia asked him to slow down so that the girls, who were seated lower than she and Mark were, wouldn't begin getting carsick. At the very top of the extinct volcano there was a coffee shop, and they ate their apples, yogurt and picked up sandwiches in the shop, overlooking the beautiful blue waters of the Mediterranean as well as the villages beyond. Their ship of course was a striking pure white crystal shard floating on that blue pond. A sight that Sophia would never grow tired of viewing.

"I can't believe we actually did this, Mark. And it's not going to break the bank," she said, leaning against him.

"Ten years, my dear. Can you believe it? Ten years

and look at these little angels. I think I'm the luckiest man alive."

Sophia surveyed the expansive view from on high. "Odds are, now that we've gotten all the excitement out of the way, all we'll have to do is just sit back and enjoy our Christmas cruise. I think we should let Teseo, and the others go after those kids. We've got a family to entertain, and that's way more important. After all, Christmas is for children. If I could, I'd love all of them all over the world, and I'd forgive the bad ones."

Mark was impressed with her huge heart.

Sophia continued. "I just want to get back to our cabin, take a nice long shower in the bigger bathroom, wash my hair, and get ready for a wonderful dinner in the dining room, with my Prince Charming and my three little angels. I'm ready for a perfect night. How about you?"

"We'll eat ice cream for dessert," Mark whispered in her ear careful not to let the girls know. "Drink hot chocolate and watch the stars show up. Then, we'll go to the theater for the fairy dust show. Then, my love, we're going to dream all night about what the next ten years is going to be about."

She kissed him as they headed back to the car.

"All the other stuff is just crap, anyway," she ended.

CHAPTER 10

SOPHIA AND THE girls came early to the dinner table, as Mark was having a short meeting with Teseo and some of his senior staff at the bridge. The Cloptons, the couple from New York, were the next to arrive, followed by the Brandon's about ten minutes later.

Mrs. Brandon gushed over how nice the girls looked tonight. "Is it a special occasion of some kind?"

"Well, this whole cruise is special for us since it's coming up on our ten-year anniversary. We are going to be redoing our marriage vows while we're here, but I don't know, today I just felt like dressing up extra fancy. And the girls are going to love the show tonight at the theater."

"Oh? You know, Kevin and I did not see the first show. Was it good?"

"Yes, they have a very talented group. We enjoyed the first one. It was a rock and roll, fifties type of dance, and the girls were glued to it, even went up on stage afterwards. Usually, they hire very good talent here."

Mr. And Mrs. Clopton vowed that they'd try to take in a show at least once. "But we kind of enjoy the casino. So, when we're at sea, that's pretty much where you'll find us," Mrs. Brandon laughed.

"And the drinks are free," Mr. Brandon added.

"I've got the girls, and they can't go in the casino, so we do other things. But not to worry, I'm not a gambler. Neither is Mark."

They were asked for their orders, the girls ordering everything off the children's menu, plus desserts from the adult list. They'd caught on very early that if they didn't like something, they just didn't have to eat it, and order something else. It was an arrangement that Sophia thought was going to greatly impact their dinners at home.

"Did you hear the news?"

Mrs. Clopton was eager to spill something. Sophia was guarded, hoping there wasn't anything about Mark that was going to be discussed.

"No, I'm not sure. What are you talking about?"

"Well, it seems someone has hacked into some of the passengers' accounts here onboard, and all kinds of people are finding charges to their accounts that they didn't authorize. If you ask me, it's those darn teenagers. And I think next time we take a cruise, I'm going to request that it be either a full family cruise, or adults only," her tablemate said.

Sophia knew that Mrs. Clopton's radar was correct.

"Do you know who's doing it? I understand there are a bunch of rowdy kids on here, not being looked after," Sophia offered.

Mr. Clopton scrunched up his nose. "They're awful. Practically knocked us over last night. They were running all around the outside of the ship, they came barreling into the theater I was told, and nearly interrupted the show. I just don't understand what parent would let their child do crazy things. It's dangerous. It's dangerous for the rest of us."

"Well, the good news is, the captain of the ship, is a friend of ours, from past cruises and from the time when I used to work for this company full time. That's how Mark and I met. But he's aware of certain individuals who are causing some problems so I don't think it'll be very long before they'll find out who these kids are, but I don't understand how they would get credit card information and room charge information."

Mr. and Mrs. Brandon were frowning but didn't have much to say. Finally, Mr. Brandon asked his wife if perhaps she should check their balance.

Sophia agreed. "Yeah, I'm going to have Mark do the same thing. When did you hear about this?"

"Everybody was talking about it in the library. And

on the buses, when we took the tour of the island? Oh my gosh, I think on that bus out of the thirty or so there must have been ten couples who had unauthorized charges on their account. They had to wait a long time before they could get somebody in customer service to help them, and they promised it would get straightened out in the next day or so."

Mr. Clopton began, "What kind of an operation is this that allows these types of things to happen?"

"The only problem I've ever had with this cruise, is years ago on one of my trips I used a brand-new credit card. I hadn't called and told the credit card company that I was going to be traveling overseas, but I had a huge balance that was available to use, and I planned on maximizing it out during the voyage. Well, I used it one time, and then the next time my card was shut down. I had a difficult time getting through to anybody in the US to get it straightened out, and I wound up having to borrow from the ship. It was most embarrassing. Now I understand to let them know in advance."

"You wonder if even that is safe," added Mrs. Brandon.

"Well, friends of ours back in New Jersey said that this is one of the safest cruise lines you could be on. And they have a very good track record as far as illnesses and cleanliness. The food's great." Mrs.

Clopton shrugged. "I guess they can't monitor everything. Life is just so complicated these days," she added.

"I agree, the staff and food and service, it's first rate," said Mrs. Brandon.

Just then, Sophia saw Mark sashaying attractively through the dining room, stopping conversations wherever he walked past a table. He smiled and nodded to those who acknowledged him for being one of the dance instructors. He gave Sophia a peck on the cheek before he sat down next to her.

"Everything okay?" she was curious to know.

Mark surveyed the table. He lowered his voice to make it difficult to hear. "Maybe we could talk about it later, but we got problems. Don't say anything yet."

Sophia's dream of a quiet evening of shows and fun, good food and conversation were in jeopardy.

"Should we leave?" she asked him, alerted to what might be happening.

"No, no. We're good for now. Not here, sweetheart. But here, we're fine."

Mrs. Clopton addressed him. "Mark, we were just talking about how some of the passengers seem to have been charged fraudulently on their cabin tab."

"It could just be an inexperienced clerk at the desk," Mrs. Brandon disagreed. "We don't want to spread rumors, do we?" Then she peered at Mark.

"You don't think the captain suspects anything like that, do you? Weren't you just talking to him?"

Mark studied her, searched the group again, glanced over the tops of the girls, who were drawing on the menus provided them, and then gave a worried look to Sophia.

"Whoa, well, I wasn't sure that information was going around. Captain Teseo is a friend of ours. As a friend, if I see something I think is wrong, I'm going to tell him. I think I need to keep our conversation private, ladies."

Sophia was confused, but Mrs. Clopton wasn't giving up.

"But you will mention this to the captain, won't you? Or I will."

Her attitude was huffy. Sophia figured she didn't like having her gossip skills curtailed.

"No worries there."

"They think it's a bunch of teens," added Mrs. Brandon.

"Yes, I understand," Mark answered. "I did talk to him about them. He's doing everything he can. Captain Teseo must maneuver his way around the different police jurisdictions as we go from port to port. But he is looking into a couple of things I mentioned others have as well. No need to panic or go spreading rumors, like Mrs. Brandon said. Let's get the facts first."

Sophia felt a bit frosty with the coverup Mark was using but gave him the benefit of the doubt. But she would be peppering him with questions when they returned to their cabin after the shows unless that was now put on hold. She didn't like that they didn't have their own table to themselves.

Mark staved off her questions, which drew Sophia's ire even further. Soon, however, she got lost in the performances and how the girls reacted to them. Even little Domenica, in her father's arms, was fascinated with the show, and bounced her upper body in rhythm to the beat of the music.

They headed down the glass elevators to the Promenade for some ice cream and to peruse the shops. Sophia spotted a group of teen boys, included in that group was a red-haired boy who matched the description of the one both Mark and her girls had seen.

"Is that him?" she asked Mark, pointing.

"I believe so. You stay near the candy store. I'll try to be right back."

When the elevator stopped, Mark took off after the boy and was soon lost in the crowd.

Sophia purchased peppermint hot chocolate since both the girls were done with candy since so much was made of the drugs in Ophelia's bag.

"I don't think I even like candy anymore," she mumbled, glumly.

"Where has daddy gone?" asked Carrie Ann.

"You know he's trying to find that red-haired boy, sweetheart. Come on, let's get you seated, and we'll wait for him to return."

After over a half hour waiting, Sophia's nerves were beginning to fray. Crowds of laughing party-going passengers, mostly without children, passed her by. Couples dressed in their eveningwear held hands. On an evening where she'd intended to have an easy-going time, her insides were feeling stretched, and sad. Even morose.

Come on, Mark.

She knew she was going to have to have that talk. Of course, he was always there to protect the innocent, but this was becoming ridiculous. The burden of most of the entertainment for the girls was left with her, while he was chasing kids like a Boy Scout. She wanted to be positive and knew his good and honorable spirit would always win out, that commitment had to also include his own family. It was not okay that they should be abandoned.

Maybe for Mark, putting himself at risk was something he wasn't afraid of and would do anytime. But for Sophia and the family, who were here to celebrate, not right the wrongs of the world, him risking his life or theirs seemed like an ill-conceived mission. Was he going to be like this the rest of their marriage together, as they tried to do the right thing for the girls? Was it right risking their safety as well?

As the girls began to stir, it was difficult to contain them. Sophia was tiring and felt exposed, vulnerable without Mark around to watch over and help. She made the decision to return to the cabin. She knew Mark would understand if he returned and found they weren't still at the shop.

She didn't want to spook the two older girls, so kept the conversation light, and tried to get them interested in tee shirts and trinkets, toys, which Domenica was hard to extract from, and the movie store where passengers could rent DVDs.

Domenica was getting heavy and needed a change. She ushered her brood into a lavatory and let the girls use two of the stalls for privacy. The toddler's dress was wet. Her tights were smeared with diaper detritus, which she attempted to wipe clean. The girls were babbling on in the stalls, sharing toilet paper and talking about the show.

With Domenica cleaned, she hoisted her up onto her hip, to take everyone back to the room. But instead of two locked bathroom stall doors, both were open, ajar, and there was no sign of the girls anywhere.

In panic, she called out. "Carrie Ann? Ophelia? Where are you?"

There was no answer.

"Girls! Come on, don't hide on me. Where are you?"

Still, there was no answer.

She checked the two other stalls. The girls were no longer in the bathroom!

Sophia darted out into the lobby area at the end of the Promenade, searching right and left.

"Carrie Ann, Ophelia? Where are you girls?" She tried it again, this time so loud, half the lobby area turned.

She spotted several clerks behind the information desk look in her direction.

"Please! Help me find my girls!"

Immediately one of the Korean crew members ran over to her.

"You have a problem, madam?"

"Yes, yes. My girls. They were in the bathroom with me, and now they're missing. Oh My God! Help me find them! Please, please help me!"

Several passengers approached, suggesting they could help, and she tried to describe the girls, but hadn't brought her regular purse with all her photos in them.

"My husband. Can you put out an announcement, have him paged?"

"Yes, yes," the clerk answered. "Let me contact the Assistant Tour Director. I'll be just one moment." She ran, disappearing into a door behind the long counter.

The crowd started to surround her, several people asking questions all at once. Domenica became concerned and then started to wail, screaming at the top of her lungs and was inconsolable. Sophia couldn't hear any of the comments.

As Domenica's tears began to flow, Sophia's did as well. She'd been searching every face she could see, looking for someone who might help, who might know, who might be talking to her girls. Did they wander off or were they—?"

"Sophia!"

The sound of Mark's voice instantly brought a combination of relief and anger. She turned on her heels, doing an about-face, and beheld her husband's worried expression.

"Mark, they're gone!" she shouted as he ran toward her.

She'd barely noticed Ophelia and Carrie Ann holding hands with their dad at his sides, trying to keep up with him. Again, anger flared. Not knowing who to blame for all the terrible things she'd thought about, she chose to unload on Mark.

"Where have you been? Why didn't you tell me you took the girls? I've been worried sick about this. This is so not okay."

But Domenica was still crying, then reaching for

her dad. Sophia then realized she was scaring the baby. Pushing Domenica into his arms, she grabbed her girls, knelt, and hugged them.

"Mommy loves you so much! But don't do this ever again. This was very, very bad."

"But we were just waiting outside the bathroom, and we saw daddy!" Carrie Ann protested.

"Do you know what I thought had happened? I thought you'd been kidnapped!"

"I'm sorry, mommy," Ophelia said, her lower lip protruding, a single tear running down her cheek. Her breathing was labored, and Sophia saw she was building up to a big cry.

"I'm sorry too. Mommy's sorry." She hugged the girls again, and then stood.

Mark was having a hard time calming Domenica down. He didn't look back at her. But he whispered just loud enough so she could hear.

"Come on. We need to get out of here. You're scaring the girls."

Sophia stopped following him to the elevator.

After a deep, cleansing breath and some courage self-talk, she blurted out, "*I'm* the one scaring the girls. Where the hell were you?"

"Trying not to get arrested."

CHAPTER 11

SOPHIA DIDN'T LOOK at him the whole trek back to their cabin. She stripped the girls down and put nighties on them, rechanged Domenica and put her into a onesie, bringing the crib in from the bedroom and setting it next to Ophelia and Carrie Ann. The girls sat in their beds, looking back and forth between he and Sophia, understanding that everything was on tender hooks, Mom was mad, and they would eventually get free of all this stuff, but they knew, they needed to just wait and behave. Which is exactly what they did.

While Sophia finished up putting the girls down, Mark changed into his pajama bottoms. He grabbed a beer from the refrigerator, walked through the sliding glass door and sat on the balcony outside overlooking the ocean. It had been another tough day, and things weren't the way they should be when he was turning in to bed. So much had to be resolved, he halfway wished that he could just stay up all night and drink. But that had been years and years since that kind of behavior had consumed him. He wished he could forget.

He knew she'd come out and talk to him eventually. He needed to just let her stay busy and take care of her babies.

Sophia wore one of his oversized cotton t-shirts with the Bone Frog logo on it, that hit her about the mid-thigh. She silently joined him on the deck, drinking a bottle of mineral water.

"I'm ready to talk whenever you want to," he offered.

"Let me catch my breath. In a couple of minutes."

They sat listening to the waves lap and crash against the sides of the hull. The moist warm air, even at nightfall, was refreshing, not to mention the calm he needed. He so didn't want to have this conversation, but he was going to have it anyhow.

He waited, and then she examined the side of his face. "I'm ready. Go for it."

"I didn't want to make a scene, Sophia, but whatever you're thinking, you need to know that I'm very sorry, and this was beyond my control."

"You're telling me, Mark, is that I have to just put up with this? I had all three girls for over an hour waiting for you in the candy shop, which is where you told me to wait. I didn't receive a message from you, you said it'd be just a few minutes and you'd be back.

You should have come back and told us or sent somebody to tell us. I was worried sick. And then this whole thing about the girls in the bathroom, I honest to God thought we'd lost them. I thought you took off to go be a boy scout and I was stuck trying to do something I couldn't control. That's the long and the short of it. And I am, yes I am pissed."

"I don't fault you for that sweetheart. But just hear me out."

"This must be one whopper of an explanation. It is unbelievable."

"It is. I went after the kid—his name is Samuel by the way, and his parents are very well respected and VIP passengers on this cruise. Not that any of his behavior is forgiven, but it's a very delicate situation for Captain Dominichello."

"So, what you're telling me is it's so important that it was worth risking the lives of your wife and your three daughters? Is that really what you're saying to me? You're right, it is unbelievable."

"Hear me out."

"Mark come on, give me a break. You're not thinking, sailor."

He felt the anger welling inside of him but of course that wasn't really directed at Sophia. It was directed at the situation he found himself in.

"Let me tell you something first that might shed a

whole new light on things. There is a possibility tomorrow on Capri I will be arrested and taken to jail. They have lodged a formal complaint."

"Who?"

"His parents. You see, I caught up to that kid, I grabbed him by the collar, and I pressed him against the wall as his friends tried to beat me down and I kicked a couple of them. I asked for help. Of course, everyone went running in all different directions— even his friends took off, and I dragged his ass into the lobby and took him to the information booth. I asked if they could page the captain, but he was unavailable, I was told. I held onto him there. I couldn't let him go and nobody else wanted to take him. I took him downstairs to the Medical Bay and left word that the captain could meet me down there."

Mark rubbed his hands together and then took another long sip of his beer.

"Fuck it all. The next thing I know, security is down there, they put handcuffs on me Sophia. I was constrained in a tiny holding cell just outside the medical bay. Where the security office is. And they demanded that I released the kid. Next thing I know, the captain and his parents are barreling through the doorway, the Mrs. screaming at the top of her lungs and saying she's going to press charges."

"Charges? For what? He was a suspect in drug selling."

"He did get a little bit of a bloody nose when I forced him up next to the wall and unfortunately drawing blood is considered assault, and it is, and they can press charges. The cruise line will not come to my aid. Captain Dominichello has to wash his hands of it because we're friends, and I have to fall on the mercy of a magistrate on Capri."

"Goddammit Mark, didn't you see any of this coming?"

"I admit, I acted hastily, and you know he's 16. He's doing things like I explained to the parents, with the pills, I explained to them that my daughter found them in the hallway after they passed by. They accused *me* of getting my nine-year-old daughter to sell drugs for me, can you believe that?"

She pondered before she answered. Mark had hope she'd understand.

"Certainly, the fact that you are a Navy SEAL, that's going to hold some weight," she answered.

"It certainly will. It also might get me tossed. I might lose my Trident."

She sat back and from the expression on her face Mark knew she finally understood what was at stake.

"They are allowed to press charges against you even though you told them about being tossed overboard—"

"They said I got into a bar fight, or I was drunk,

and I fell over. I have no proof, and I don't know who did it, but I did push the kid up against the wall and I did bloody his nose. That little asshole stood there smirking while I was getting reamed by this ridiculous woman."

"Who you're going to have to be very nice to Mark. So, we go see the consulate in Capri. There must be a US consulate on the island."

"There isn't. We'd have to go to the mainland for that. But I can maybe get somebody from the Navy to come in and help get a JAG officer or something. Teseo has the drugs, but I'm not sure he's going to release them. He just wants the whole thing to go away and he's pretty disgusted with me."

"I can understand that. In a way, you jeopardized his captainship. Or am I getting this wrong?" she asked.

Mark didn't have an answer for that, merely shrugged his shoulders, repeating the you-stupid-son-of-a-bitch-self-talk in his head. He realized that he'd allowed his emotions to get the better of him. Because it involved his daughter, because it involved drugs, because he'd been tossed overboard which made him feel ashamed and could have caused him some serious medical issues, because they're riding rough shot on all the other passengers, picking on the innocents, he felt he was battling in a situation with both hands tied behind his back.

"Mark, they released you, and that's a good thing. What did Dominichello say?"

"He told me to go and stay in my cabin, that we are not to join the group tour of Capri, until further notice. I'm under cabin arrest for a while unless I want to spend the night in their jail. I'll stay here with you and the girls thank you. And then he said we'd have to sort it out in the morning."

Mark was going to elaborate further but thought better of it. Sophia caught onto this and asked him.

"What is it that's going on? I don't understand how you, a Navy SEAL, could be questioned and doubted going up against the parents of a teenager who obviously has been acting up this whole cruise so far. You are a decorated war veteran still an active-duty SEAL, and you'll never raise children who will behave so despicably like their son. You didn't start this. I don't see why that won't hold credibility for you tomorrow. I just have a hard time thinking that they would let the word of two strangers override your reputation and what you do for a living. And the fact that it put your daughter in danger, well what father wouldn't react like that?"

Mark decided it was going to be no use. He was going to have to tell her the rest.

"Well, the complication, Sophia, is, she is the

daughter of the Secretary of Defense. The *Italian* Secretary of Defense. And her husband, is the new ambassador to England. They were headed from Italy to England to start his new post, and taking the cruise was their way to celebrate his new appointment. It's the very beginning of his new career, but she's so well connected, there isn't anybody who's going to touch my defense, not from Italy anyway. They're saying the whole family has diplomatic immunity. I'm just hoping Uncle Sam decides I'm good enough to defend me. And frankly, it was a dumb ass move on my part. This whole thing has been horrible. And we haven't even started finding out how the drugs got here and whether they really belonged to this ambassador's kid. But my money says yes."

"I agree with you."

He was encouraged when she took his hand and placed it up to her face, pressing it against her cheek.

"Somehow, sweetheart we'll get through this. This isn't supposed to happen to us. Something's come off track. We'll find it."

He was relieved, yet disappointed he'd let everyone down.

"Sophia, I love you even more now than I did this morning. Thank you for putting aside your anger and listening to me. I'm going to need your support. Thank you so much. I'm going to fight this every way I know how."

"No Mark. There you're wrong. We're going to fight it. All of us. We're going to do it together."

CHAPTER 12

THE KNOCK CAME on their cabin door at 7:00 a.m., and two uniformed officers from Capri stood in the hallway to greet Mark when he answered.

"I'm afraid you're going to have to come with us."

Sophia stood next to him. They had discussed what might happen and was certainly happening right now.

"I'll just get my clothes on, and can I bring some things?" he asked the officers.

"You can bring some toiletries and a change of clothes if you like, sir. However, you will probably not be returning to the ship."

Mark turned to look at Sophia, and she could see he hadn't anticipated this.

"We are traveling with our three daughters, gentlemen, and I am also employed by the ship, so is Mark, as a dance instructor. We've signed a contract."

"Which is null and void if he's found guilty of manhandling a minor. We have put in an inquiry to your U.S. Navy, and once we are assigned someone, we will let you know. But you have two choices, ma'am. You can stay on the ship with your daughters by yourself, or you can come to Capri with us. He will be housed in the local jail downtown in the city center. You will have to arrange accommodations."

Sophia swallowed hard. She knew Mark was going to suggest that she call Kyle and as soon as she was out of earshot of the local security officers, and she couldn't wait to do so.

"Gentlemen, just give us five or ten minutes to get the girls dressed and for us to get dressed as well and we'll accompany you. I do have luggage—"

"If you want to come with him, you need to leave your luggage behind."

"But—"

"I'm sure the captain will make sure that all your things are collected. Just bring something you can put together in the next five or ten minutes, and then you must come with us. We have a police skiff waiting to take you all to the island. Your arrangements with the cruise line as far as any reimbursement or remuneration is not of our concern. He needs to be held until a determination is made as to whether or not charges are going to be filed."

They woke the girls up gently, got them to put on pants and T-shirts. Sophia packed their day bags, and cleaned out the little refrigerator, tossing in all the yogurts, fruits and healthy snacks that were stored there. Then she packed her own bag and added it to Mark's.

"Make sure you bring some reading material. We're probably going to wait long hours until we get answers," Mark said.

"Once we get you situated, I'm going to give Kyle a call, or is there someone else you need me to call instead?" she asked him.

"No. Tell him I'm going to call him as well, and I'm assuming we'll get the name of an officer in charge here. Kyle's going to have to give that to the Navy. It sounds like they haven't pressed charges yet, but it's imminent."

With several hundred passengers watching the police vehicle leave the crew bay, heading for the island, their family among the four other uniformed officers, Sophia was glad she couldn't recognize anybody or see their expressions.

"HEY SOPHIA, HOW'S it going?" Kyle asked her.

"Well, this is a phone call you never thought you would ever get from us, but Mark's been arrested, being held for roughing up a minor on the cruise ship."

"Geez, that doesn't sound like Mark at all, what happened?"

Sophia explained to him the drugs that they found, the accusations about certain things like how the boys had been basically getting into trouble since the first day on board and explained who his parents were.

"I see, I really do. That's not a very enviable position. You are not staying on board, is that correct?"

"I'm not leaving Mark. We can always stay nearby and that's the next thing I'm going to do after you hang up. But I need to know what kind of representation we're going to get here, if the Navy can help out, or if I have to get an attorney myself to help represent Mark."

"I don't know how that works; I just know the command will probably send someone over to look at the case file and help him strategize a defense. You can probably start by making a list of all the sympathetic viewers on that cruise. We want somebody who can vouch for what you guys were doing there, and I'm real disappointed to hear about Captain Teseo's decision. But I'm understanding that perhaps he has no choice in the matter. Not if he wants to stay employed."

"Do you think he will find a way to help us?" she asked.

"I'd bet on it. But he won't do it publically. He's a good guy."

"That makes me feel a little better. What should I do next?"

"Honestly, Sophia, I'd start looking for an attorney.

I'll see if I can do some research for you over here but see if you can get someone good in Italy. I'm afraid you'll need one. At least temporarily."

Kyle promised to get back to Sophia with some contact information, and he also mentioned that he would be having their team liaison reach out to her.

"If you want to bring the girls back to San Diego, maybe that would be better. I'm sure we can take care of them here, so you can focus on helping Mark. I'm not so sure having all of you over there is a good idea."

Sophia had not thought about that and frankly thought it was a good idea.

"Do they have State Department representation on Capri? Are they familiar with how these proceedings go? And one other thing Mark was wondering, if the parents have diplomatic immunity, does the kid have that too? What if he's the one supplying the drugs?"

"That's all above my paygrade sweetheart. Just tell Mark not to worry. Is it okay if I tell the team, or do you need to check with Mark about that first?"

"Yes, go ahead tell them. Who knows, maybe that group will know somebody."

"Sure thing. You take care of those beautiful ladies in your care, and we'll fill the holes where we can. Now I've got some calls and work to do."

"Thanks, Kyle, and I'll think about your offer with the girls. It might help us all concentrate if I had less distractions."

The Old Savona Hotel had been one of their stays during their honeymoon. From the hand-painted china to the "smoking room" that now allowed women and cigars, to the finely feathered beds and silky sheets, it transported her to happier times, when her whole future was in front of her.

She put it all out of her mind and tried to remember how it felt to be newly married to her Prince Charming, when the whole world was not big enough to express her love for Mark.

Her evening prayer at starlight was that she could feel that way again, but this time do it as a whole family of five.

"God, we don't ever leave anyone behind. He never does it. I'm certainly not going to do it either. Like the SEAL motto, Only Easy Day was Yesterday, yesterday was indeed easier. But tomorrow we're going to start to fix it."

CHAPTER 13

MARK WAS TOLD he'd be transferred to another facility. His guard told him he'd be kept out of the general criminal population, and he was told confidentially by one of the senior officers transporting him, that it was being done for his own safety, and out of respect for the fact that he was a United States citizen.

"I've not been able to telephone anybody. My wife thinks I'm at your port station. How are they going to find me?"

He knew things happen when an individual member of any of their teams was transported to somewhere and where the police were not being forthcoming with where and why and what was the timeline he was facing. While he didn't suspect he was the victim of foul play, the longer this went on, the less confident he was that his own government, the Navy, or even Kyle or Sophia, could intervene on his behalf.

It would be useless to fight, and yet it was not like him to just sit and wait until he'd been victimized.

"You are not to worry my friend, we are a law-abiding country here, and our police force is the finest anywhere. I am just doing my duty. And if you do not resist, I am sure you will find the new accommodations much better for your interests."

"I want to know who ordered this? I didn't ask for it. Did my attorneys, or the consulate or the Navy request this?"

"I am not privy to all that information sir. It will be revealed in time. I am just given the duty of getting you safely to the regional holding center. It is not a facility that is large, nor will you be placed into a large population of ordinary criminals. First, you are a US citizen, and you have certain rights. Second, you are a member of the armed forces of our allies, and we treat our friends as we would want to be treated in your country."

It didn't make any difference to Mark; he was still worried.

"Can I just have a phone call then?"

"Not until I am directed that it is okay."

He had made the comment to Sophia to bring some reading material, however it looked like he was going to be the one needing the reading material since there was nothing he could physically do about his situation. They told him he could bring an extra set of clothes and personal items for toiletries, but that bag never made it into the car, which scared the shit out of him. Was he just going to be taken somewhere to be done away with? And surely, the new ambassador to Great Britain, even though his son was an asshole, surely, he would have some say over what would happen to him, and no matter what, there would be repercussions. It was hardly the type of action that warranted an international incident. But Mark knew very well that that didn't always make a difference.

He was thinking about this whole situation. It was his fault that he'd reacted so strongly with the kid. He regretted that. In hindsight, his normal patient self should have jumped in, and he could have restrained the boy who was not his match in physical strength, without causing any harm, and certainly without causing bloodshed. But once blood was spilled, it seemed to set in a whole new set of rules, and what might have been considered a harmless encounter or misunderstanding, suddenly became a full-blown assault and battery.

He was concerned about Sophia. She was stuck in Italy with all three girls, their cruise was ruined, their anniversary was ruined. And it was entirely possible that Mark's career was ruined as well. Of all those things, he knew whatever he needed to do to make it right, even if it cost him his career, he would apologize and do just that. But he needed to know Sophia would be safe, that they could get back to the States, regardless of what happened to him.

He wished he could talk to her, he wished he could let her know that at least he was not rotting in a rat-infested cell with a bunch of low-level criminals, or worse, drug dealers or murderers. He had no idea how the criminal justice system worked in Italy, although he had nothing to necessarily think negatively about it. He really didn't like the fact that he didn't seem to have any rights as a detainee, almost as if they were treating him like a terrorist as his country did. Now he knew exactly how they felt.

When he asked Sophia to marry him, this was not at all what he envisioned. He knew there would be dark days, there would be difficult times, married to a Navy SEAL, and he thought he'd prepared her well for all the possibilities that could occur. But never in his wildest dreams did he ever guess that something like this would happen. And wouldn't it just be his luck, to be the one to expose some new danger. It seemed like every day their team members had to be more and more careful about what they said, what they did, their public persona, and the media attention. Some had written books, some had gone on speaking tours, been outspoken about all sorts of things including politics.

None of that was anything Mark ever wanted to do. He was just trying to protect his family. And he knew that somebody on that cruise was dealing drugs. He wanted to stop it before somebody died unnecessarily.

There was no crime in that.

It was the source of his frustration. His actions were taken for the good of everyone. Not for his own personal benefit, although he did allow his anger to take over.

That he regretted most of all.

On a normal day, he could have looked out the window and appreciated the beautiful little tiled villages, the switchback streets and cobblestones, the happy commerce of vendors and marketplaces they passed. They loved the culture and the countryside in Italy. That's why they'd chosen to be there for their honeymoon. And Sophia, being raised here, with an American father but an Italian mother, loved her country as well. She became an American citizen because she wanted to for Mark. She could have held onto her dual citizenship forever if she'd wanted to.

But Sophia now was going to experience a second tragedy in her young years. Her father had been killed in the military, and her mother moved them back to Italy, back to her family, upon his death. So, she'd been uprooted twice, and now she was having to spend her time with three children, worrying about Mark's welfare.

He hoped she had it in her to stick with him. But if she decided she'd had enough, if she blamed him for all of this and couldn't forgive him, whatever it is she wanted to do, whether she wanted to go back to live in Italy and not have anything to do with the SEAL Teams or the military or the United States, he would let her do it. He loved her that much. If she honestly thought it was better for the girls, he would go along with it. He'd try to fight, but he'd go along with it.

The hardest thing in the world was sitting and waiting. He had told her this repeatedly. He's said it to his LPO Kyle. No, he didn't do wait at all.

The town of Montepulciano was atop a hill, sort of an artist community, with many large villas, olive trees and vineyards. He remembered this little village when they were on their honeymoon and had spent several afternoons there walking through the shops. Stayed at a villa in Imprunetta and walked the olive orchards in the evening at sunset.

Today, it looked dark and foreboding. A solid rain had started, and unlike the coastal area, since they were inland quite a way now, it was dreary. The rain-washed cobblestones glistened and steamed in the afternoon sun. Every person he saw on the street, every driver that passed them on the road, were strangers. There was not one friendly face the whole trip.

They had handcuffed his wrists, but uncuffed his ankles. But when he got there, no doubt he would be doing a perp walk, for whoever's benefit it was that he was transferred. Or if they drove into some tunnel somewhere and there was no daylight, well, Mark knew what that might mean. Maybe we were just going to stash him away somewhere and lose him. Claim nobody knew what happened to him.

The wait and the trip were killing him.

"So, am I going to be charged please? I adhere to a very strong code of conduct, it's very likely that this whole situation is going to end my career as a Navy SEAL. My wife is in the country and she's Italian by birth, with our three daughters, not knowing where I am. If anyone is trying to get a hold of me to help me, they aren't going to find me unless you give me information or allow a phone call."

His driver, the medaled officer in full dress black uniform, stopped at a stop sign. Mark could see a large prison-type structure up ahead.

"We are almost here. This is a special facility, for very high value assets, some military, some political, and yes, some spies. Very famous prison. But you will not be registered in the general population, as I have told you several times. You simply must wait. And once we process you and put you in your room—"

"Is it a room or a cell?"

"I am not supposed to promise, but I believe that it is like a dormitory. It is the facility where some of our ministers and high-profile businessmen are held while they serve time. It's not like your vision of what a full-on prison would be. But it is fortified, because through the years, there have been attempts at certain people's lives. So, it's quite safe. You just need to be patient. And I will make sure that the authorities here know what your desire is, and that you need to speak to your wife, or your commanding officer. So, I can help you, who is your commanding officer?"

"His name is Master Chief Kyle Lansdowne. I'm with SEAL Team 3 based out of Coronado, California. I have been a Navy SEAL for twelve years, and I have never had a blemish on my record."

Mark decided not to reveal to him several of the ops where there were certain questions asked about his performance, but that had been straightened out, and as far as he knew nothing was negative on his record.

"So, this Officer Lansdowne, is the person you wish to speak to or your wife?"

"Both of them. And he's Master Chief Kyle Lansdowne. I need to speak to both. Sophia my wife doesn't know what to do because she is not an attorney. But she needs to help me find somebody to represent me. Kyle Lansdowne is the person in charge of the entire team, and he's going to be grilled by the Navy as to what happened to me. They aren't going to just stand by and allow this to happen. And I don't understand why it even is."

"Navy SEAL Mark Beale, I sympathize with your situation, but again, I must tell you, you have to be patient and let things work out as they do. I am not your enemy here. I am only the person who is driving you from point A to point B. It was determined that this would be a safer place to put you. I must trust that decision. I'm sure you will be one of the first to know if anything else develops."

They had stopped at the sentry gate just ahead of the two-story archway leading inside the prison. Rather than having building upon building of cells, the central area was a courtyard, complete with a garden, including an herb and vegetable garden. This surprised him. The perimeter of the facility looked like office buildings, and in one wing, which was about four stories tall, there were bars on the windows. It did look like it was a holding facility, but he didn't see any prison yard, and gardeners working on the garden were dressed in white, looking more like chefs than gardeners. There were heavily armed men at the sentry, and opposite the courtyard a second exit with large steel doors that could roll back to accommodate a large truck or equipment of some kind. Those were locked, and a sentry posted in two barrack houses on either side.

The driver stopped at a wide stairway. There was a metal and glass intricate overhang which shielded anybody from rain who exited their vehicle to walk inside.

The driver uncuffed him.

"No shackles?" Mark asked.

"No sir, if you will please walk behind me, cooperate, there will be no need for that. I want you to just follow me please and we will deal with the desk duty officer."

Mark rubbed his wrists which had become raw from the handcuffs, and slowly walked up the steps to the double doors into a rather ornate lobby area that could have been the inside of any of the nicer Italian hotels. The floor was exquisitely patterned with tiled inlay work, wrought iron balconies overlooking the lobby area from the second and third floors. Statues of various military figures, angels, and busts of several favored Italian patriots. Mark recognized a few. One was a bust of Garibaldi, and several other military conquerors he had studied in his classes.

The day desk was up another two steps, was nearly 20 feet long and was made of white Carrara marble. The woman behind a glass shield sitting at the desk lowered her glasses and greeted the driver.

"He is to be placed in the conference room first, you may leave as soon as our liaison takes charge."

She was an attractive woman in her forties, with hair spun up into a French bun, her uniform tight, and she looked like she was all business.

"Ma'am—"

His driver tried to interrupt him.

"It's okay. Let him speak please," she said.

"Ma'am, my wife is half-Italian half-American. We were on a cruise—"

"Yes, Mr. Beale, I'm aware of your circumstance."

"She doesn't know I'm here, and I need to speak to her. I have not been permitted one phone call yet."

"We are aware of this. All in due time. I believe the arrangements are being made now. If you please follow your driver down the hallway, he will show you to a pleasant interview room, and we will get you some water. Are you hungry as well?"

Mark was famished, more from nervousness than anything else.

"Maybe some fruit, some bread? But mostly I need water. Thank you."

"Do you need to use the facilities?"

Mark looked over at his driver and frowned.

The man nodded. "Yes, I have to accompany you, I have to watch everything."

That pissed Mark off big time. "Yes, I will need to use the facilities. And if I may ask one more thing, I brought a change of clothes, and some personal items—toothbrush and deodorant that sort of thing. I don't believe they came with me in the vehicle. Will I be given a chance to wash up?"

"Once you get to your permanent room, you will be provided with prison-approved attire, and your personal items. Ricardo, would you please show Mr. Beale the restroom please?"

Mark took it as a good sign that they were going to allow him to use the regular lavatory off the lobby area, which might mean that they didn't consider him a dangerous criminal. He walked behind Ricardo, entered the men's room, and took a long pee. He washed his hands, and whispered to his observant driver, "This is fucking insane. I've never had anybody watch me do this. You would think I could get a little bit of privacy."

"Not until you've been searched. But they're going to speak to you first it sounds like."

As he washed his hands and dried them, Mark added, "Ricardo huh? Where I come from, we have a famous actor Ricky Ricardo from Cuba."

"My father was Cuban."

Score one for intuition. "So how did your Cuban father get to Italy?"

"He was protesting. Arrested, did his time, and was released. That's when he met my mother."

Mark was stunned, not knowing what to say.

"You see, Mr. Beale, you are not the only one with a checkered past. We sometimes don't always choose the path we get here, but if we follow the rules, life turns out. I think I'm an example of that. I've had good fortune. And I have it because I play by the rules."

CHAPTER 14

SOPHIA HAD WAITED all morning for a call from Kyle or the Navy, or even Mark himself. Without getting through to anyone, she had taken the girls downstairs to have breakfast, trying to soak up the time, while she devised her plans.

She needed to find an Italian attorney and was hoping that Kyle or somebody from the Navy could point her in the right direction. She didn't want to just pick somebody or ask the hotel manager for a recommendation, since this could be a criminal manner, and it involved immigration and political issues. The longer she didn't hear from Mark, the more she worried.

She was trying to stay calm, trying to stay present with the girls. How did women in war torn areas hold it all together? She wondered about this. Now she knew how it felt. Nobody around her to help her, all the men in her life she normally counted on for protection, were gone, and the roles were reversed, she was supposed to do something to help Mark, whereas normally it was the other way around.

Sophia knew that if she could just concentrate and think, she'd be able to sort out what was the right path forward. Just like she'd seen Mark do in the past, she got out her notebook and started making a list of all her questions.

Number one was what were the rules for detaining a non-Italian citizen? Were there circumstances where a US serviceman was arrested in a foreign country, and what were his rights, and what would the military do to help him? She figured that it probably depended on the country.

Getting her computer out, she Googled several topics, and didn't find anything but advertisements for attorneys for people trying to stay in the country. But nothing mentioned about international or immigration convictions for battery or assault. She knew it was an advantage that she spoke fluent Italian, because of her heritage, so she could make those calls, but she didn't trust that information would be helpful.

"Where are you Kyle, and Mark? Why haven't I heard from you?" she asked herself.

Finally, she packed the girls up and hired a driver to take her over to the detention center in Naples.

Domenica was being stubborn today, and she fidgeted in her arms, so she set the toddler down and gave strict instructions for Ophelia and Carrie Ann to both keep an eye on her if they were all in the same room. Domenica caught onto this little game quickly and began running back and forth, screaming, and giggling, and annoying the officers who were working the front desk. She barely got three words out before she'd have to turn and reprimand her kids.

She looked into the eyes of one of the officers who appeared to take pity on her and begged him.

"I'm looking for my husband, Mark Beale. He was brought in here early this morning. It's noon, and I have not received a call from him nor a call from his superior officer, or anybody in the Navy. Can you please tell me what's going on? And is there any chance I could see him?"

In Italian, the policeman explained to Sophia that Mark was no longer in the facility.

"Excuse me? Where has he gone? And how come we were never told this? I'm staying at the Savona Hotel just a few miles away, why wasn't I told that he'd been moved?"

"I believe someone is in the process of getting in touch with you, but it was decided that he would need to be moved to a more secure facility."

"A more secure facility? You mean like a regular prison instead of a holding area?"

"Yes, it is a prison. It is about two and a half hours

away, in Montepulciano. You know this town?"

"Yes. Again, I do not have a car, we've been of-floaded from a cruise ship and all my luggage has not arrived yet, and nobody has called me to help me find an attorney to represent him. Surely there must be protocol here. May I speak to your commanding officer?"

The gentleman she'd been speaking to had an immediate change of expression. His warmth evaporated, and a cold blue icy stare substituted it. Sophia became worried that there was something planned for Mark that they didn't want to reveal to her. She began to get hysterical. Her lower lip quivered as she felt her will crumbling.

Two women officers came out into the lobby and helped to occupy the girls so the entire front office could think straight. Sophia was about to have a meltdown of major proportions, but she knew she had to keep it together for the girls. On tender hooks, several times she shouted out a command at the girls, which was not like her normally. But the stress level was driving her nuts. The uncertainty of Mark's position also felt like she was trying to climb out of a pit of quicksand, making no headway, and with nobody in sight to rescue her.

"So, where is this facility? Can you name it for me?"

The officer in charge handed her a piece of paper

with driving instructions to the prison, and suggested if she wanted to save money, she could take a bus.

"I'm not going to take a bus with my three girls and no luggage. I'm supposed to be getting return calls. This is ridiculous. I'd be better off to stay in the hotel. At least there, I'll have food and a place to sleep and can change diapers. I just can't pick up and travel and I have no one to watch the girls."

"Do you have relatives nearby?" he asked her.

Sophia thought about her mother, but that was going to be out of the question, as well as her brother. If she could get ahold of the ship, and get permission to come back on board, at least there would be facilities there to entertain them, but at this juncture that was going to be impossible.

She took the directions given her, thanked the ladies for helping with the girls, and asked for a taxi to take her back to the hotel. One of the women officers offered to take her back in a police vehicle, which she accepted.

Exhausted, hungry, and tired, she leaned against the door to their room and broke down crying. She slid down the back of the door, until she sat in a ball on the floor tucking her knees up, pulling her arms over, and sinking her head low.

Little Ophelia came over to her and gave her a hug.

"Mommy? Where's Daddy? He needs to help you,"

she said.

"Daddy is in a meeting and I'm trying to find out how to reach him. I'm not having any luck and I'm very upset. And I'm so sorry, I need to get some help, but I'm striking out as far as finding the right person."

"Why don't you call him?"

"Because he doesn't have his phone, sweetheart. He's not allowed to take calls in his meeting." She smoothed over Ophelia's sweet cheeks and gave her a kiss.

"Thank you, sweetheart, for caring about Mommy. I promise this will all be over soon."

Domenica ran over to her and gave her a hug as well. Carrie Ann was a little more cautious approaching her mother.

"When are we going to go back on the boat?" she asked.

"Well, plans have changed, and I'm afraid we are not going to be going back there. This important meeting Daddy has meant that we all had to leave. I will know more as soon as I can reach someone. So, until then, we can stay here, or we can go downstairs to the pool, whatever you like."

"I don't have my swimsuit," said Carrie Ann.

"Neither do I," said Ophelia.

That's when she decided to give the police a call again, complaining about the lack of luggage.

The hotel front desk knew that they were expecting a delivery to be brought to her from the ship but noted that they had not received a call and were not expecting that delivery today.

"I need a favor, if you might. Since our luggage isn't here, is there some place I can find some cheap swimming suits for us? A second-hand store nearby? I'm not prepared to spend the money at your hotel store, if you understand what I mean."

"We have a lost and found, and at the end of the year, we donate these clothes to charity. Let me see if I can find some suits in there. People are always leaving them behind. Not worth contacting the guests to try to mail them. You're welcome if that meets your approval."

"That would be lovely. Thanks so much. Do I—?"

"Give me a few minutes and I'll bring what I have up to your room."

"You are very kind."

"Will you be staying one or two more days, or longer?" the desk clerk asked her.

"I'm not sure yet. I will know more in the next twenty-four hours. If you get any indication that the luggage or our personal effects are arriving, would you please call me or text me on my cell?"

"Absolutely."

The clerk paused, then added, "You know that tomorrow is Christmas Eve. We have a special dinner here at the hotel, in two seatings so that guests can attend the candlelight children's choir. It's a tradition here in Naples. Can I put down a reservation for you?"

"I'm afraid I'll have to do something less expensive. But thank you for thinking of us. Is the church very far? Can we walk, and is it safe?"

"Very safe, and only four blocks away. You'll find lots of other parishioners going as well."

"That sounds lovely. The girls will love it, I'm sure."

"And about the dinner, let me see if my manager can approve the four of you being our guest tomorrow. I understand your Christmas has been impacted. I don't want you to think all of Italy is unfriendly. I'm sorry you are going through this, and I'm praying for you."

Sophia called Kyle's number again and got a recording. Then she kicked herself for not having called Christy before but did so now.

"Oh Sophia, I heard all about it from Kyle. You must be beside yourself. I can't imagine going through all that." Christy said.

"Well, I'm hearing nothing, and I feel like I should be interviewing attorneys or getting instructions from our State Department or someplace. I don't know what to do and now I'm told that Mark has been moved. He's in a facility that's about two and a half hours away up in the mountains. I don't understand this. Is he being taken away for some solitary confinement? Has he been charged with anything? What do I do? We don't have any luggage. I'm using credit cards for this hotel, but if I don't need to stay here, if I could go to a cheaper place—Oh my gosh, Christy, I'm beside myself and feel so powerless. I want to do the right thing, but I need something I can accomplish. Do you understand?"

"Yes, I do. I really do. And I'm going to get all over Kyle for not getting back to you. Have you tried calling Teseo, the captain of the ship?"

"I don't have his number. Can you get that for me? I'd be happy to call him. I need a referral for an attorney. I could be meeting with attorneys, I could be strategizing, I could be helping get petitions going so we could try to intervene here and get him released. But I just don't know the first thing about this."

"Let me see what I can do and either I or Kyle will call you back. Have you heard from the Navy at all?"

"No, I have not. Wouldn't they reach out to me? Isn't that standard procedure?"

"It usually is. My worry is that they may not be tuned into everything that's gone on. Perhaps it's just a question of them getting up to speed."

"But meanwhile, Mark is further away from me, I have no contact with him. They're not allowing him to call me, and he could be in great danger, and there's nobody on his side to help. I just feel like a fifth wheel here and then I've got all three girls."

"Well, if you were here in California or could get on a plane back to California, we can help you with that. But I'm not sure you want to do that. It's going to feel like abandoning Mark. I must tell you, Sophia, if this is a long, protracted situation, you probably are best to come back home, get them into a routine they're used to, and the wives will help. There's no problem there. It could be very expensive if you wind up having to stay there the whole time. And I'm sure they'll allow you to come home."

Sophia hadn't even considered that perhaps Mark's family would not be allowed to return to the United States.

"What kind of a world is this?"

"I think it's an unusual situation. From what Kyle has said, and I know he is looking into this, because of the involvement of the new ambassador to England, things must go through channels, and until the right people get together and start talking, nobody in the rank and file in Italy, is going to touch this. I'm sure once we figure out what's going on, there will be a solution presented. But try to keep calm, and I know that sounds flippant, but your best asset is if you stay calm and you stay clearheaded. In your shoes, I don't think I'd be as coherent as you are. We're tough, but there is a limit to what we can live with, isn't there?"

"I never expected this. I didn't even know all the ins and outs of what happened. But we'll get to the bottom of it. Please have Kyle call me."

Sophia thought about calling her mother but knew it would just upset her. She decided to call Devon Brandenburg who had married Mark's best friend, Nicholas Dunn. It was approximately eight hours ahead in Italy, so it would be early in California, but this was important enough that she hoped Nicholas and Devon would forgive her for calling before sunrise.

Nick picked up on the first ring.

"This better be good, or I'm going to ram this phone down your throat. Who's calling at four o'clock in the morning?"

"Nick, it's me, Sophia. Mark's been arrested in Italy. I am beside myself. I'm stuck in a hotel in Naples. We've been taken off the ship for our 10-year anniversary cruise, and I have all three girls with me. I'm trying to get through to somebody at the Navy. Kyle's working on something, but I just wanted to call somebody and brainstorm a little bit. Do you know anybody in the Navy or the State Department who could maybe give me a hand?"

"Geez, Sophia. Why was he arrested?"

"It's a long story, Nicholas, but the long and short

of it is he caught some kids he thinks were dealing drugs and it turns out one of the kids' parents are headed to England, his father recently appointed the new ambassador to England from Italy. I guess the complaint was made because Mark confronted the son, who is a minor, and while he was restraining him, gave him a bloody nose, and the guy's mother just completely freaked out. They pressed charges or going to press charges, and I need to get an Italian attorney or somebody from the State Department or the Navy to intervene."

"I understand. Is Mark innocent of this?"

"No, he did get angry with the kid, but it happened because he was trying to restrain him. And the kid was struggling. He was trying to take him to the authorities, so that he wouldn't be selling drugs to other kids or adults on the cruise ship. He tried to protect the passengers. But unfortunately, it's being portrayed that he beat up a minor."

"Yep, that sounds like a clusterfuck all right. And the Navy's not going to like this, Sophia. You got to be prepared for that."

"Listen, we'll take whatever they dish out. The main thing is, I need to make sure that Mark's okay. And I can't reach him."

"I know that we have friends up in Portland and there's a former State Department liaison who is related to our friends, perhaps Kelly can intervene, but I'm not sure. It needs to go through Kyle though. See what he has to say first."

"Yes, I get that. It's been five hours now and I haven't heard a thing and when I tried to go over to visit him, that's when they told me that he'd been moved. They did that without consulting me. And they took us off the ship without our luggage, so I have nothing. I just feel like I'm being treated like a criminal as well and it's not fair for the girls either. I mean, is that going to be the next thing they're going to say the girls must go somewhere else because I'm a criminal like Mark? I'm just grasping at straws."

"Now, there has to be a logical explanation. You just keep yourself and the girls occupied. Let me see if I can make some calls. I'm not going to promise anything, but I do promise I'll get back to you. And listen, if you need to talk to someone, I'm sure Devon, when she gets home, would love to call you back."

"Devon's not there?"

"No, she's down in LA, at a training seminar. We're branching out into the Airbnb business, ecotourist. This a license that she wants to have for operating our facility here. She'll be back day after tomorrow. Otherwise, I'd put her on the phone now. But you take care and I've got this number and what happens when you try to call Mark?"

"I saw them take his phone. And they have his passport, and I really don't know what he has with him, but there's no contacting him. But I would gladly appreciate a referral if you can find someone."

"Will do. I'll spend the entire day if I must, making calls and seeing if I can help. You just hang tight. I'm so sorry this is going on, and you know if I must fly over there and give Mark a hand, I will. He is my best friend. I know he'd do the same for me."

"Thanks, Nick. I really appreciate this."

"If I do come over, then I'm going to have to make arrangements for my kids, but we've got family in the area, so it's not like what you're going through. It will take me a day or so to arrange all that. But let me see what I can do, and I'll try to call you back before you go to bed tonight."

Sophia was slightly relieved, but decided she'd stay proactive. She could follow up on the luggage, calling the cruise line, she could follow up on the luggage with the police department. She did both. Crossing those off the list, she was told that a delivery was expected before the end of the day today, and that the bag that Mark had packed for himself would also be returned to her. His other personal effects, like his cell phone and his passport, would not be returned to her until further notice.

With the suits the clerk delivered to her room, including a new one for her from the Hotel store, she took the girls downstairs to the indoor swimming pool and decided to put everything out of her mind and give herself just an hour of swim play. Her phone was nearby however, but it was more important that she give time to her girls.

About five o'clock in the afternoon, as they were returning to their room, Kyle called back.

"How are you holding up, Sophia?"

"How do you think? So, what's going on?"

"Well, we have a problem. I believe Mark is going to be charged. It's a difficult situation, but I have someone from the Navy Special Investigations, who's going to reach out and get you a referral in Italy. The one thing that we don't want, is to have this appear in any media because that will complicate the whole thing. It's a sensitive negotiation, must be taken through the proper channels, and needs not to get distorted. I'm sorry to ask you this, but you're probably going to have to be prepared to be there for a day or two, maybe a week."

"Oh my God. This is getting expensive. But Kyle, whatever it takes. We're here. All of us are here."

"I think that's the right thing to do. And we'll find out about why he was moved; I wouldn't necessarily disagree with the officer who told you he was being moved for his own protection. That's very like how they do things over there. The last thing in the world they want is for him to run into problems in jail. That certainly would cause an international incident. So, if the news media doesn't get hold of the story, which means you must be quiet about all of this, we'll just let channels take care of themselves and hopefully everything will be ironed out. I'm not going to be able to promise that I'll have an answer tonight, but I promise to call you in the morning if not. Are you okay? Do you need anything?"

"No, I'm fine. Thank you. What about calling the captain? He's a friend, isn't he?"

"I've already done that. I'm working on something there. But you just need to stay put and stay calm. Your job right now is to be level-headed and be able to react very quickly if something's needed. Again, I'm so sorry. The fact that he hasn't been charged and a court date set, that's all-good stuff. So, let's try to be positive about it, and we'll see what kind of miracles we can make."

"Yeah, miracles. Is this going to mean the end of his career?"

"Let's handle that if it comes up to it. Let's hope it doesn't come that far. So, I'll talk to you probably in the morning. You be strong, Sophia. I know you're strong. Mark is counting on you."

"If you get a chance to talk to him, will you tell him we're here, and we're not going to leave him behind. I don't care what I must do, Kyle. I'm going to get him out one way or the other."

Kyle chuckled. "Yeah, I thought you'd say something like that. You're just like Mark is. He'd do the same for you. How are the girls holding up?"

"They're good. I'm going to find a babysitter recommended by the hotel. They have licensed services here, and I think I can trust them. Then if I must do the drive into the country, I can do that. I just don't want to take them all over Italy. It's hard for me to do that with all three of them."

"I understand. You work on that and let us do our job on our side. Keep looking up. Keep praying and having good thoughts."

"Thank you, Kyle."

"Thank you, Sophia. You're one hell of a woman. Thanks for supporting your man. He's worth it."

CHAPTER 15

ARLA GUALTIERI, THE regional prosecutor, sat
down across the table from Mark.

"Special Operator Beale? I am going to ask you a series of questions about the incident that's been reported to us. It's a complaint. And I'm going to ask your indulgence to give me absolutely the truth, no matter what you think I might have of that. I need to get to the bottom line of what exactly occurred. Can you do that?"

"Absolutely. I've been waiting to have my chance to tell my side of the story. I'm completely innocent."

"This is going to be your side of the story; you are completely innocent?" She lowered her glasses on her nose and stared at him with her huge blue eyes, drilling a hole all the way to the back of his skull.

Mark shrugged, with eyes downcast, said, "Well, that's not entirely true. I did push the kid. I pushed him up against the wall so I could grab onto him. I was fighting off several of his buddies."

He raised his eyes to try to determine whether she believed him. His opinion was inconclusive.

"How many of his friends were trying to stop your actions?"

"Three, maybe four. I'm not sure. I tried to fend them off as best I could by kicking and grabbing onto the kid and trying to reach them with my other hand. I was outmatched, but I didn't want to let the boy go. I was told his name is Samuel."

"Yes." She peered at the paperwork in front of her. "Samuel Collazo? I understand his father is taken on a position with the Italian government and will be residing in England."

"I didn't know who his father was. But my daughter was exposed to what I believe to be drugs, that dropped out of Samuel's pocket. She tried to return it to him. She thought it was candy—they were looking like a fruity cereal, multi-colored rings, she thought he'd want it back. They either didn't hear her or ignored her, so she kept it, and she put it in with her bag of candy we had purchased earlier."

"Was she exposed to these drugs?"

"No, I think I would know that. She said she didn't. And we were with her the whole time. When she described Samuel to me, I started looking over the ship to see if I could find him, and I ran into him that night."

"Did your wife hear your daughter describe Samuel?"

"Yes, she did. So did my other two daughters."

"Okay, and what did you do with these supposed drugs?"

"I gave them to the Captain, Teseo Dominichello. He is a friend of several of us on our SEAL team. We have been on cruises where he's been on board before."

"Yes, I understand there was a terrorist takeover of one of the ships in this Italian line? And you and your team were able to crush the takeover?"

"Yes, although the official story, is that the passengers overtook them. We weren't really supposed to be there, or be involved, but the passengers did assist us in finding the terrorists and holding them so that they could be arrested."

"Okay. That's a tall tale, Mark. May I call you Mark?"

"You can call me anything you like, as long as I can get out of this place as soon as possible."

"And why do you think you should be released?"

"Because I think this kid is a problem. I think he's not been supervised, allowed to terrorize some of the other passengers on the ship. He's an accident waiting to happen. If he's got drugs on him or dealing drugs, it's something that should be stopped."

"And you took it upon yourself to do this?"

"Unfortunately, yes, I wanted to make sure he was apprehended, so an investigation could be done, and possibly he could be removed from the ship. Instead, this is what happened, and I'm here and he's on the cruise. My entire family is in Italy and pulled off the cruise, my wife and three daughters, and he is allowed to run around freely on the ship and he's a danger to any other child or adult on that ship if he's dealing drugs. I don't know if his parents know about his activities, but I believe I was arrested so that they protected their son."

"That's a pretty damning assessment of their moral code, wouldn't you say that?"

"Yes, I'm well aware of the fact that parents some-times don't supervise their children as they perhaps should. Or have a different opinion of what's accepta-ble and what's not acceptable. I can see how they would be concerned that having a son who deals drugs or is in possession of drugs, could jeopardize his father's opportunities. I'm not sure I would've done anything different had I known how connected his parents were, but I knew that he needed to be appre-hended. And I thought I was doing my job to protect the innocent people on the cruise."

"Does your Navy talk to you about interfering with other government's judicial system, their laws, not inserting yourself since you are not sworn police or prosecutors? You are operators, you go in and handle riots and defend and rescue people in war torn areas of the world. But this is Italy, this is a civilized country, with a constitution and a court system. You defied the authority of the security on ship as well as the police and the judicial system here in Italy. This is a very serious offense."

"I understand and I'm very sorry for my actions. I probably overreacted."

"Probably?"

Shrugging and leaning over the table with his hands folded together, he added, "Yes, I overreacted, I should have been more careful not to hurt him, I was solely intent on making sure he was captured, and I should have paid more attention to the fact that I am stronger and bigger than he is, and I should have allowed other people to do their job. But that's the worst of it. I was doing it for all the right reasons."

"But if you thought someone was going to harm your family, would that give you the right to murder them? To cause a great deal of physical injury?"

"Under the circumstances, these circumstances, no. I made a mistake. This mistake could cost me my job, I could lose my trident over this. I was angry at this young boy's actions. I'm angry that I'm being charged or being charged for something that I really didn't intend to do. I am angry that my wife and children are not able to talk to me, that I'm not able to have representation or talk to my commanding officer or the naval liaison or anyone from our State Department. It appears that all my rights have been removed and Samuel's rights—well he's allowed to run free and do whatever the heck he wants to do. It hardly seems fair to me. But that's your determination not mine."

"You say the captain of your ship is a friend of yours? Why didn't he intervene?"

"If I had an answer to that, I would give it to you. I didn't even get the opportunity to speak to him. I was told by the security team that I had to remain in my cabin, and after I gave him the drugs, I no longer had any communication with him. Just because we are friends, I would've thought I would be given more choices. I was moved to this facility because I was told it was for my benefit. I don't understand any of this, nothing's been explained to me, and it just seems that I was the victim here. Granted, I used perhaps more force than I should have, but I'm the real victim. And there are going to be other victims if he's not apprehended. That is something I'm most concerned about, and I suppose Captain Dominichello is focusing in on that. As he should."

"So, what do you think should happen from here on?"

"Well, if I've caused battery of some kind assault, I will have to pay the consequences. Whether it's justified or not, that's your determination not mine. I didn't mean to cause him harm. I just merely wanted to apprehend him."

"But what is it that should happen in your opinion?"

"In my opinion, I should be released. I also think a team should be sent to the ship to investigate the drug use, to interview the boy and his parents, and to determine perhaps by interviewing other passengers on the ship, if the boy and his friends are in fact a nuisance to other passengers. I know that there are people we talked to who complained about those kids. I have their names. If you like you could interview them. I think after you investigate what went on, you'll see that I'm telling the truth. I'm not proud of it, but I'm telling the truth."

She looked at Mark without revealing any emotion. She asked him about his family, his upbringing, what his specialty was on the teams, how long he'd been a SEAL, how long he intended to remain in the military, and he answered all her questions. By the end of the interview, Mark was not sure if he was believed.

"Are you going to charge me with an offense, officially?"

"I haven't determined that yet. I do need to speak

to the parents who lodged the complaint. Of course, it's going to require that they leave the ship to come here for the interview. That may be a problem for them. We will do our best to investigate, in the meantime though, you are going to need to stay here. I will allow reasonable use of phones, you'll be housed in an individual room, by yourself, and your meals will be delivered to you. I'm not going to place you in the general population or allow you to have communication with other prisoners here. If what you said is true, I don't believe a lengthy stay, or international incident should be created over this. But it's very important that we get to the bottom of why it was that you were so angry at this boy and verify that he either is or is not dealing or possessing drugs. Like you said, if he is a danger to the other passengers, we are concerned about that, and we need to do something before they leave Italian waters."

"They're supposed to be in Capri all day today. I believe they're supposed to head out in the morning for France. I think the next stop is Nice."

"I will contact the captain immediately, and I will ask permission to come aboard to conduct a cursory interview if the passengers are unable to come to us. But I will ask that this be done before they sail further. I'm sure the captain is not going to want to delay the cruise. But it is going to be his decision."

"Well, I thank you for listening anyway, and you

can look up a couple of passengers there, Mr. and Mrs. Clopton, and Mr. And Mrs. Brandon, both of whom discussed with us their displeasure with this band of boys that seemed to run into everybody and cause problems. I'm sure there are others as well, but we did discuss it at length."

She handed Mark a business card and wrote her cell phone on the backside of it. "You may be receiving visitors our government might arrange for you, an attorney to help represent your interests. Please have him contact me directly before he speaks with any other members of the police force or the prosecutor's offices, please. It will be to your advantage that he does so."

"Thank you, ma'am. Now, can I call my wife?"

"Yes, I believe we are arranging for a phone to be brought in here, and you may give her a call now if you wish. I will also allow you a call to your naval representative. We are going to need their help in sorting all this out as well."

Mark was heartened. There was a tiny glimmer of hope burning in his chest. He prayed to the god of SEALs that if he were able to escape this situation relatively unscathed, that he would devote the rest of his life to his family, his wife, and kids, even if it meant he had to give up the teams. Whatever it took, he'd made enough mistakes in his life. He wanted to make sure that he kept Sophia and the girls part of it. It was the most important thing in the world to him.

Nothing else even came close.

CHAPTER 16

THE SUITCASES WERE delivered to Sophia's room, and much to the delight of the girls, they began dressing up in some of the new clothes they had brought with them for the cruise. The little time they spent down at the pool had refreshed everybody, and even though it wasn't normal, life had sort of returned that way, temporarily.

Her cell phone rang with a number she didn't recognize, and when she answered it, she was ecstatic.

"Hey, sweetheart. It's me."

"Oh my God, Mark!" She was speechless, bumbling, tears brimming over her cheeks. She felt like she was going to pee in front of her daughters.

"I'm good, and I just have a couple minutes to tell you I love you, and they allowed me a couple of calls. How you guys holding up, sweetheart?"

"I've been worried sick. We've not had any news. You say everything's okay? Are they going to release you?"

"I wouldn't go that far yet; I haven't even talked to anybody else. I'm not sure what the strategy is, or if there is one. But I didn't want you to worry. I think this is a safe facility, and for whatever reason they decided to house me here I'm grateful. I'm in Montepulciano—"

"I remember it so well, Mark. It's such a beautiful little town."

"Haven't seen much of it, since I'm in the prison, which apparently is a high-level, not exactly maximum-security prison, for government and corporate offenders. I'm not even sure whether there's anybody who's done serious crimes here, but it's a little bit like a hotel, except there are bars and I have to wear the prison uniform."

"Do you have any chance of talking to Kyle or an attorney, or have they explained charges? Or if there will be?"

"I'm not sure. And I may have to ask you to get hold of Teseo. We may need his help."

"Kyle said the same thing. I know he's trying. He gave me the number. I left a message."

"Oh, that's good, I'm glad you've talked to Kyle. How did he sound? I'll bet he was a bit pissed about all this."

"Not sure about that."

"Is he working on something? Because I haven't

heard a damn thing."

"I just spoke to him today around noon. That's the first he's heard of things. It takes time. But yes, he promised me an update later tonight or tomorrow morning. I talked to Christy as well. And I hope you won't be angry with me, but I also called Nick Gunn. He said if he had to, he'd come over here and help you break out, that was a joke."

"That was funny, but we can't do that here on these lines. It might get construed as something else. It looks like there are several things being put into motion. I sure would like to talk to an Italian attorney. And I have concerns about using anybody that they might recommend to me here, so Teseo and Kyle those are going to be our best bets. Since you speak Italian, you can interview them and kind of get an idea what they're about, and perhaps by then they'll let you see me. But I just don't know who to trust. You should be careful too. But I wanted you not to worry and—"

"Daddy!" Carrie Ann had overheard Sophia's conversation with Mark. All three girls ran over to grab their turn at the phone. It was a shoving match, eventually the phone winding up on the floor and scooting to the other side near the sliding balcony door.

Sophia rescued it before it went into the street below.

"Sorry about that. The girls are so excited. They

keep asking for you, and they don't understand every-thing. We're all concerned. God I'm so relieved to hear your voice. You sound good, really good."

"Where are you staying?"

"I'm at the Savona Hotel, you remember it, it's very nice. They have invited me to sit in on a special dinner tomorrow night for Christmas Eve. And the hotel clerk has been wonderful, found some bathing suits for us until our luggage arrived."

"Oh, your luggage did come? Any idea where my bag is?"

"Yours and my bags came with the luggage as well. No worries there. Anyway, we're going to go to the candlelight vigil and the children's choirs at the cathe-dral that's within walking distance from here. It's a custom in Naples. I think it'll be nice, and if you're back, I would love nothing more than to have you join us. But in the meantime, we're going to have that little slice of Christmas anyway."

"Love you so much, and you're doing such a great job. I'm just waiting for instructions. One of the things that is going to be important is investigating that kid, before they leave Italian waters. I believe tomorrow is when they head out for France. I'd like to get some representation or get hold of Teseo before that hap-pens."

"Yes, Kyle said the same thing. I'm sure they're doing everything they can. Do you need anything? Is there anything you need me to verify? Papers, anything at all that proves who you are?"

"I have my military ID and my badge, they know who I am, and they have my passport. I think it's something else that they're waiting for. But we'll get there. I just want you to know how much I love you and how much I'm thinking about you and how much I wish I could be there with you. If this turns out to be a long event that will take days or weeks to resolve, I want you to go back home, and muster up the resources we have there, rather than spending time here waiting for answers that just don't seem to be coming. I'm sure they're doing everything they can."

"One thing Kyle said is that it was important that the media not get hold of this story. I guess that's more a warning for me than for you."

"He's thinking about the SEAL community. I'm not worried about my career, Sophia. If it happens it happens. I know Kyle's probably worried about it. But if the media gets hold of it, in my way of thinking, it would be more a blemish on the new ambassador to England than it would be on me. I would think they wouldn't want that. But I'll let them tell me I'm wrong."

"That's a good point. And I think I agree with you. Well, I'll be here. You make your calls, and if there's anything else I can do, please text me or call me or have someone else leave me a message. We're safe, people here have been wonderful, and the main thing is I'm just trying to give the girls some Christmas spirit," she whispered into the phone. "They still think we're going back on the ship."

"Gotcha. Well, I love you, and I'll be in touch soon."

"Love you as well."

"And Sophia, things are going to change. One thing I've been doing is thinking about things. I'm partially responsible for all this. I should have made a different choice. From now on, I'm going to do things different-ly. You'll see."

"You try your best."

"This time, it wasn't good enough. I got distracted, and I put you all in jeopardy."

"Lots of time in the future to talk about that. For now, just get yourself out of there. I want you home. You belong with me."

"I sure do. I'm going to make that my sole priority. I promise."

THE HOUSEKEEPING STAFF brought back their washed, ironed, and folded clothes, and Sophia asked for a recommendation for pizza, which had been the choice of the girls. She showed Sophia a brochure on the desk with the phone number of a pizzeria that came highly recommended.

Sophia ordered an extra-large pizza because she was feeling like she could eat the whole thing herself, she was so relieved, and famished. She put a movie on for the kids, prepared, a bottle for Domenica, after she managed to smear pizza sauce all over her pink cheeks. Resisting being washed, the toddler finally settled in for the night with her bottle, the girls next to her in the hide-a-bed.

Sophia double-checked the lock on the door, and then took a quick shower, getting ready for an early bedtime. She was glad that so far, the news was good, now she needed to rest. Tomorrow they'd start putting together a team and a plan. God, she hoped Nick and Kyle and Teseo and all the rest of them, all her friends and Mark's brothers forever, would come to Mark's aid. She wondered if she should attempt to stir things up a bit with the ambassador and his wife or ask the local police if they were looking into the drugs on board the ship but decided she would let others do the work they were better at anyway.

The girls were asleep, the TV was turned off, Sophia grabbed the toddler, brought her to bed with her and promptly fell asleep.

At 2:00 a.m., her phone rang again.

"Sophia, this is Teseo Dominichello, and I understand Mark has been transferred. Forgive the early morning call."

"No, it's okay. We expected him to stay here so that's where I am. But he's in Montepulciano, at the federal prison there."

"Yes, I know of it. I have some acquaintances there. You must be beside yourself with worry."

"That's good of you to say Teseo, but Mark is the one who needs your help. I need an attorney that I can go visit with and can give me some direction on what we should be doing, if there should be petitions filed since I don't understand how the system works here."

"You best just leave things the way they are, since sometimes things happen unofficially. I think he's in good hands, although the ambassador and his wife are still forcefully demanding charges be filed. The main reason for my call is just to let you know that so far, the prosecutor has not decided to charge. But that could happen at any time."

"That is good news. I will take any bit of good news I can."

"Well, there is one other thing, and I hesitate to let you know, but they have made a complaint against not only Mark, but Carrie Ann. And that's a whole other issue. Family court—anything having to do with minors, is a very tricky situation here. If they don't become reasonable, and I'm sorry I couldn't appear to be coming to your aid, but if the ambassador and his wife don't turn their thinking around, I may have to ask you to do something your attorney probably wouldn't recommend."

"What is that?"

"I'm sorry, I'm not at liberty to say. But you'll know when I call you. I'm only going to ask you to do this if we've lost any other leverage we have. Just understand that. Everyone has Mark's welfare at heart. If there's a way to get him back soon, rather than have this drag on for weeks and months, that's what we're going to do. I am meeting with Kyle via Skype tomorrow. We are not going to pull out of port until I know exactly what we're running into. The ambassador and his wife are demanding that we keep to our timetable. We'll see what happens."

"Thank you, and I appreciate your cooperation. I wasn't sure."

"No, my dear, Mark is a dear friend and you, well you light up the whole ship with your smile and your dancing. I just want to get you back doing that again. I just know this must be extremely difficult. So, I will pray for you, please have heart, and we'll talk probably tomorrow in the morning."

"I'll talk to you whenever you call, but I'm going to need a few hours to catch up with my sleep. Thank you so much for calling, Captain."

MARK WAS AWAKENED early by the sounds of shouting and arguing coming from down the hall. His room was a square ten by ten, with windows facing the garden he'd driven past yesterday. Bars of course made it impossible for escape, but the door had a window in it, but was not set up with bars like a normal jail cell.

It was also temperature controlled, he was given an adequate pillow, and two blankets. He also was issued disposable slippers and a set of prison fatigues that turned into pajamas and were reasonably comfortable. He was allowed to turn the light on and off, although there were rules on when he could do this, and with no blinds or shades on the window, as soon as light came in, his room was extremely bright—he would have to say even cheery.

He'd been dreaming about something he couldn't completely recall. He was in a boat, a small boat, like the rubber boats they used to practice with during BUD/s training. But it was a holiday, he felt the bobbing of the water, lulling him in and out of sleep. But when he heard the arguing, he bolted straight up.

He didn't understand Italian, so the conversation was meaningless to him. There was an older gentleman who was dressing down two or three other people. He did hear several times the word "general," so he assumed that there was some military component to the argument. Then he heard the distinctive words

SEAL Team 3 from Coronado. That's when he knew the argument was about him.

He had not been able to get hold of Kyle but left a message. He was given a phone number Kyle could call back on—the cell on the prosecutor's card. As far as he knew, no one yet had contacted the Navy.

The argument got extremely heated and then another individual arrived, putting an immediate stop to it. There was whispering, and then the entire group left the hallway off into a more secure, quiet room.

Mark decided to wash his face and put on his clean set of prison fatigues. The razor he was given was dull, and he wasn't given shaving cream but a bar of soap, which was of good quality. He felt better with a clean face and shave. He smelled better, and his clothes were clean. He set aside all his toiletry articles and sat on the edge of his cot, slipping his feet into the slippers. It was time to wait.

The books that he had decided to bring never made it to him. But he was glad to learn that several of them, signed copies from admirals or men he had learned special warfare tactics with, were not lost. Those were some of the most important books in his library, which was small.

Finally, he heard footsteps coming down the hall. At the same time, he thought it odd that he didn't hear any other prisoners, at least in this part of the building.

He was going to ask about that.

He saw the face of one of the guards, in the window. Keys jangled and the door was opened. Behind him stood an older gentleman in a full military outfit, not a dress uniform, but more a uniform of a politician with medals and ribbons overflowing. It reminded him of all the medals and epaulettes he'd seen on the cruise ship officers. Rounding out the group of three was the female prosecutor he had met with yesterday.

"Special Operator Beale, we have a request for an interview. You can refuse the interview if you like, but we are going to encourage you to meet with General Verasco, who is the grandfather of the boy you assaulted on the ship."

The guard was very serious, showing no sympathy and no emotions.

Mark studied the older gentleman and sized him up to be a blowhard, a fat, opportunistic, politician throwing his weight around. He didn't trust him at all. The lines of his face formed a perfect scowl.

"I wish to be told first when I am going to see my representation," Mark insisted.

The prosecutor came forward.

"Mark, as I told you yesterday, we are working on things. I don't have an exact answer for you, we are attempting to get in touch with your commanding officer, and the Department of the Navy. We have reached out to the consulate in Rome, and we understand an official should be coming here today. One way or the other, you will have somebody from your side of the aisle visit with you. I'm not sure what that means yet, but we will try to get some answers for you."

"Okay, so if that's a promise, is it something I can count on?"

The general boiled over quickly, showing distain and a total lack of respect. "You have no right to demand anything. You have assaulted my grandson" he said.

"Not to be disrespectful, general, but in our country, we are innocent until proven guilty. I have not had a trial, and I have not as far as I know been charged. I am looking forward to my day in court. I'm sure everyone wants to get to the bottom of what occurred. Probably me more than anyone else." Mark saw that his delivery pleased the prosecutor, who stifled a small grin.

"So, let's proceed down to the interview room where we can sit at the table then," the guard inserted.

Mark held his hands out as if he was going to have handcuffs applied, and the prosecutor waved him away. "It's not necessary Mr. Beale. You're being detained, but not charged at this point."

He followed the group of three down the hall to the same interview room he'd been in the day before. He was given the seat at the head of the table. Everyone was given a bottle of water. He didn't realize how thirsty he'd been.

The general leaned into the table and folded his fingers together in front of him. "You are a trained killer, Mr. Beale. You have learned how to subdue and attack your enemies. You are no match for a 16-year-old kid, who may not understand how lethal a weapon you are. But I understand. I understand the threat to my grandson's life."

Mark considered whether he should reveal too much of what he thought would be his defense. He decided to give him just a tease.

"I saw your grandson break the law. If I am convicted and go to jail, I'm going to see to it that he does as well. He put my daughter in danger, and he knows it. I suggest you get the truth from his parents."

"This is ridiculous. What justification did you have for bruising his face and perhaps breaking his nose?"

"I didn't break his nose. Believe me, I know what the sound of a broken nose makes. Show me the medical report, will you?"

"He was treated at the medical bay. But I will get you the records if you like."

"I need to have that for my defense. I also would like to have him examined by an independent physician. Not on the ship, but in Naples."

The prosecutor interrupted him. "Mark, I don't think we can ask for that."

"You need to check your priorities Ms. Gaultieri. You almost sound like his own counsel. Your job is to see to it that justice is done. Nothing more."

She smiled, but Mark could see it was brittle. "I respect your opinion, general. That is exactly what I'm focused on, as we all are."

Mark could see that no further good would come of the conversation. Perhaps this is what they'd been arguing about. But he couldn't sit and listen to any more of it.

"Why do I have to sit here in this facility unable to appreciate my wife and three children, the youngest who is barely walking, my daughters who don't understand why their father, a war hero, is being treated so despicably. I am shocked that I am not given the same rights as your grandson. It is not the way you would be treated in my country."

"You think your country is so great? Your country has lots of problems, my son."

"I am not your son, I don't know anything about you, but I do know that your grandson takes drugs and sells drugs, and for that I believe Italian law is quite harsh. Now perhaps your grandson is too young to serve in a detention facility, but then shouldn't his parents be held responsible for his behavior? There are several people on the ship who will bear witness to some of the things that gang of boys was up to. They were not just having a good time, they were bumping into people, they were stealing things, they were kicking bottles around on the deck until they broke, and I believe one of them pushed me over the railing. These are dangerous boys with substances that kill people. I'm surprised as a leader in your country that you're not even halfway concerned about that. I'm surprised that the new ambassador to England isn't concerned about finding out who had the drugs and why."

The older gentleman was clearly disturbed by Mark's remarks.

"I believe general, it would be a good idea if your grandson and his parents came here to sit for an interview. I have some questions," said the prosecutor. "Perhaps that could go a long way to sorting everything out."

"That's preposterous. They're on a cruise for my son-in-law's new career in England. He's on official state business and they have diplomatic immunity. They are not required to appear anywhere."

"I don't believe that covers the sale of drugs in international or Italian waters. I have spoken to the captain of the ship, who has verified that the contents that were purportedly dropped by your grandson, contained the chemical fentanyl. Do you understand what a serious allegation that is?"

"This is why my daughter has complained that this gentleman here has put his young daughter up to selling drugs to earn money on their cruise. This is why it's so important that he'd be prosecuted."

"If it's warranted, that is exactly what we'll do. On the other hand, if we find evidence bearing out Mr. Beale's statement of facts, we are going to have to open an official investigation. Perhaps the British government may have to be notified of this."

Mark was glad the prosecutor said what he dared not say. He did not know that Teseo had made contact. Things were looking up, but he wasn't out of the woods yet.

"I am going to cooperate 100% with any investigation you wish to have Ms. Gualtieri, and I assume that General Verasco, will do the same. I'm at your disposal."

CHAPTER 17

"**A**RE YOU SITTING down, Sophia?" Kyle Lansdowne asked her.

"No, I don't want to sit down. Is it good news?"

"I think it is. We found you a top-notch Italian attorney, who's a law professor in Milan. He's agreed to take on your case pro bono, and he knows several of the players and has represented international soccer stars and businessman who have been detained in Italy on a whole host of situations from visa issues to extraditions, sanctions, and prisoner swaps."

"Music to my ears, Kyle. I knew you'd come through. Any idea why all this crap is happening to Mark?"

"Sometimes grudges are formed, cabinet ministers and officials throw their weight around and create havoc for foreign nationals who get victimized and caught in the crosshairs. I believe he is exactly the guy you should have."

"Okay, so when does Mark get to see him?"

"Well, he would like to come pick you up in about two hours. If you can get a sitter for the girls—"

"I have one already arranged. Just in case. So, two hours, that makes it 10:00?"

"Yes ma'am. He will pick you up at the hotel, and the two of you will discuss the case as he's driving you up to Montepulciano. Teseo was able to get permission for the three of you to meet. Mark of course has to agree to all this, but I'm going to call him next and tell him to start making some notes if he can, they've told us they're going to give him pencil and paper so he can start working on his defense."

"What about charges? Are there going to be charges?"

"Our hope is that there will be no charges filed and the whole thing will just go away. However, we still have the issue of the drugs, and once the two of you and your family are back home in the States and on base, I believe Teseo's company is going to go after the grandson of General Verasco. But that's a little bit out of my hands. In the meantime, the kid and his family are going to be pulled off the ship and will be sent to London for his new job appointment. The company does not want that family on the cruise ship any longer."

"Wow, so they must have talked to some of the

people we talked to then."

"It was reported by several people that someone was dealing drugs. Teseo has every single account, however your little bag of tricks that Ophelia had, is what's really driving this case. It is complete evidence, and if the baggy and wrapping and other things are put into forensic analysis, we're certain that his fingerprints will be all over it. I think they're going to be in a lot of trouble. But my main concern is getting you guys out of the country."

"Well, I have the babysitting taken care of, and I was going to attend the dinner here at the hotel, then we were going to go up to the cathedral and listen to the children's Christmas Eve service. So, are you sure I'll be back in time?"

"We'll make sure of it. I think you're going to like this guy."

"What's his name?"

"Antonio Garibaldi. Turns out he's a distant relative of the famous Garibaldi who is credited with uniting the Italian country as one. It's a long story, but an interesting one. I have a couple JAG officers here that have spent a lot of time with this guy. I think he's, our man."

"Thank you so much."

Sophia quickly raced down to the desk and inquired about the babysitter who had been arranged for a future date. The clerk was a new girl Sophia had never seen before.

"Can she watch the girls for just a few hours this afternoon? I have to go see my husband."

She checked paperwork. "I see it here. I will call her right away. And you said you were meeting someone? May I have a name in case they come looking for you?"

"Antonio Garibaldi."

"And what time do you need to leave?"

"He's picking me up here at 10:00. So, I would say from 10:00 until maybe 3:00 at the most? I fully intend to be back in time for the dinner, and the candlelight vigil."

"We will have her show up at the room at 10:00."

The babysitter arrived early, which Sophia was grateful for. The girls were given books to read and told that there would be no TV until they finished some writing exercises that Sophia had given them. And she had asked them also to draw a picture of their adventure in Italy.

"When are we going back to the boat?" asked Ophelia.

"Not this time honey, but I promise we'll do another cruise someday. This time, something else came up that was unexpected. But it's all going to be okay, so don't worry."

Sophia waited for the attorney down in the lobby.

At five minutes before 10:00, the gentleman arrived. Bringing an umbrella, he parked in the front and walked straight over to Sophia.

"You are Sophia Beale? Mark Beale's wife?"

"Yes sir, and you are Antonio Garibaldi?"

"At your service, ma'am."

Sophia stood, hoisted her computer bag over her shoulder, waved to the clerk at the desk and exited the front of the hotel. Garibaldi held the umbrella for her and opened the car door. He had a small new Mercedes coupe.

With all the rain, it was difficult for Sophia to recognize the roadway, but as they traveled, she saw the distinctive peak of the village of Montepulciano and the three churches, and one castle perched on the top like crystals. They were still more than 45 minutes away, but the peak of the extinct volcano, which had shaped the area, could still be seen for miles around.

"So, Kyle says that you have a lot of experience with immigration, or foreign businessmen and their issues with the government, similar to what Mark has here. I understand you're from Milan?"

"That's where my office is."

"And where you teach."

"That is correct, ma'am."

He was impeccably dressed. His nails were buffed and trimmed, his haircut looked fresh, and the interior of his car was immaculate. Sophia had always liked the attention to detail some Italian men adopted. Even his shoes were well polished and there wasn't a speck of lint on his dark charcoal gray raincoat.

"Why don't you tell me in the few minutes we have left here, what is your defense, Sophia? What is it that you are going to be wanting to present or you want me to help you present."

"Well, first of all, the boy was in possession of drugs, and we saw this. My daughter saw it, and I understand the captain has had the substance tested and it tested positive for fentanyl. I guess Mark's defense is going to be that he was acting for the good of the passengers, even though it wasn't his job. He's just wired to protect the innocent. He especially has a hard time dealing with people involved in the drug trade or human trafficking. I think what happened to him is his reflexes just kicked in and he overreacted a little bit. Like he was on a mission with his SEAL team."

"I was not aware he was a SEAL."

"Is a SEAL. He's still active. Didn't you talk to Kyle Lansdowne, his LPO?"

"Yes, yes I did."

Sophia wondered if she'd heard Kyle correctly but put it out of her mind. "What else do you want to know?"

"I think what you have is a good start. What about

Samuel's parents? Had you run across them before? Did you have any confrontations on board ship?"

"I don't believe we have. We heard from several people that there was a band of boys running around misbehaving. We also heard that there had been a rash of hacked accounts on the cruise line, charges from the stores or the liquor store added to somebody's cabin bill. Our table mates said on a tour they had taken that several people on the bus had been hit with fraudulent charges. Also, with the percentage of elderly people on the cruise ship, the way those boys run up and down the hallways, and the outside decking, it's dangerous. So, I think it was something that Mark thought was important enough to act quickly. He did not intend to cause him any harm, certainly not to draw blood."

"I'll need the names of those witnesses, or people who had their accounts hacked."

"Happy to do so."

"How did this escalate into Mark's arrest?"

"He hasn't been arrested. He's been detained."

"Pardon. Yes, detained."

"The boy's mother went crazy, accused Mark of really battering Samuel. I didn't see him of course, but from what I understand, it was just a simple bloody nose."

"Ah, but blood is blood. If he draws blood, there are certain rules and paths going through our criminal justice system, that must be adhered to. Was anyone present who saw the altercation?"

"I don't know the answer to that because I wasn't there. I know that the boys' friends probably were there, because Mark told me they were trying to interfere, trying to pull him off Samuel, and they were punching him and kicking him while Mark was trying to hold Samuel and stop him from escaping."

"Okay, so we're going to have to find witnesses if we can. That will greatly improve our chances."

"So, what is your strategy going to be?" Sophia asked him.

"Well first, I think there is a gentleman I work with who has some questions, and he's sort of an expert witness, so if you'll indulge me, I'd like to pick him up on the way."

Sophia was slightly concerned for this new development and wasn't a hundred percent willing to take on another stranger in the vehicle.

"That wasn't the arrangement. Will the prison allow another person?"

"It's no matter, if you're uncomfortable with it, we can do it another time. But I just thought it would help us get to the bottom of Mark's situation."

"If you think it will help Mark, if you think that they will allow Mark to have three visitors instead of just two, I don't see where it would hurt. Who is this person?"

"Ah, he is a forensic accountant. I use him when we

are discussing cybercrimes of various natures. He may want to ask you about your banking, about your income, that sort of thing. I guess what we're trying to do is show a pattern that you're law-abiding citizens, you don't make a lot of money, you're not interested in selling drugs. You don't have a background or a history of that and you have no ability to manufacture the cybercrime of fraudulently charging other people's bills. We must create the groundwork of reasonable deniability; we need to make sure that the judge in this case sees that you are the least likely people to be involved in anything like that. And perhaps to convince him as well, that this is the type of crime drugs, credit card fraud, that young teens often find themselves involved with. That's a pattern that we're looking for."

"But I thought the main issue was the bodily harm, the assault charge?"

"What we're facing here is multi-faceted. We want to be prepared."

"I think Mark would be all right with that. Is it very far out of our way?"

"No, not really. Maybe ten minutes."

Sophia sat back as he turned off the two-lane country road leading to Montepulciano and followed the signs toward Florence.

"We're going to Florence?" she asked.

"No, we're stopping before there, but it's in the same direction."

"So how long is your normal winter break then?" she asked.

"Winter break?"

"For school. You teach at the law school Kyle told me. How long do you have off between semesters?"

"We break the end of November, many of the students go skiing in winter. We come back and start the semester the first of February. It's customary, however, for students to take summer classes, so in a way we have a nice vacation the beginning of summer, and then again in the middle of winter around Christmas. Are you a religious person, Sophia?"

"Oh gosh, that's a difficult question. I was raised in the church, but aside from special performances and weddings and funerals, Mark and I don't really attend. We may be reconsidering that decision."

"And how do you like Italy? Is it your first time?"

"You know I am half Italian. My mother is Italian. My father was a serviceman killed in combat when I was young. We lived in California at the time, but after my father's death my mother moved back here. I've been raised in two cultures, and Italy is not really what I consider home, but it is my family's home. I consider California home to us now."

"You ever considered living here as opposed to living in the States?"

"You mean going back to work for the cruise line? Or opening a dance studio, something like that?"

"Yes. Raising your family in ancient cities of Europe, is a great cultural experience. Don't you feel unsafe living in the United States with all the crime?"

"I guess up until this situation with Mark, I always felt safe. He was always there with me. I never had reason to doubt my safety. I guess I took a lot for granted."

They continued driving, following a narrow roadway that barely had room for one car. On several occasions they had to pull over onto a muddy shoulder to allow opposing traffic to pass them. The beautiful rolling hills and vistas of olive trees and vineyards disappeared, and they came through a section of land where it was heavily forested. At last, they drove up to a large estate home, with an automatic iron gate that opened when the Mercedes stopped just in front of it.

Sophia extricated herself from the car just as the attorney was rounding the front side to help her. She had her computer case strapped over her shoulder and he showed her the way to the front door. They were greeted with an employee in a uniform, directing them toward the living room.

"This individual is very wealthy, I take it. What is his relationship to you other than to use him as a consultant?"

"We are colleagues. We work together on many things, but it can be said that I work for him as well."

Sophia examined the tall ceilings with oil paintings depicting military men, some with metal armor, showing life as it was perhaps two or three hundred years ago. There were pictures of horses and portraits of beautiful women in flowing gowns, hired portrai-tures done by professional painters. The interior was filled with antiques, beautiful glassware, a collection of crystal goblets and whiskey glasses to one side, vases, china teapots, and vintage spirit bottles behind leaded glass cabinet doors. There was an assortment of clocks mounted on the mantel piece over the fireplace. It was a very masculine room, obviously set up to impress, which it did.

"This is quite a place."

"This house has been in their family for nearly four hundred years. They are descendants of royalty in a way," he said.

Sophia checked her watch. "I certainly hope he'll be down here soon. I don't want to worry Mark by making him wait."

Behind her, Sophia heard shuffling, and then a deep booming voice saying, "He's going to have to wait, my dear. We have some questions for you."

She whirled around on her heel and saw an older

gentleman in sweater and slacks, appearing to be close to her mother's age.

"You must be Sophia?" he asked, holding out his hand.

"Yes sir. And I'm sorry I didn't catch your name."

"General Verasco. I am the Deputy Secretary of Defense. We are discussing the way your husband abused my grandson."

She must have flinched, because the general added, "I'm not your enemy, Sophia, I just would like to make sure that proper justice is done."

Sophia stared at the attorney who avoided eye contact in return. "What's going on here? Are you an expert witness helping us with a case? Or is this something else? I feel like I've been lied to."

General Verasco began again, "I want to impress upon you that it would be wise for you to settle this particular matter outside of the authorities. If we must pursue a trial, if we must pursue what my daughter would like, which is have your husband charged with assault, and perhaps have a very public trial, it's going to be expensive, it will take a lot of time, and I'm hoping we can circumvent this."

"What is it you want from me?"

"There have been some allegations made against my grandson that I need to have corrected."

"Sir, I'm not the one making the allegations, it's my

husband who saw the drugs, who turned them in, those items are outside of our control. They've been given to the captain, and I believe that's all been turned over to the police already."

"On the contrary, I have it on good authority that the drugs are under lock and key and will not be allowed outside the police station unless there is a very good reason why. In the absence of evidence, you really don't have a case."

"What exactly are you getting at? I feel like my husband should be part of this conversation. And don't you think it's wrong for you to insert yourself before I've even had a chance to talk to my husband after he was taken away? This was our ten-year anniversary gift to ourselves, we're traveling with three children, we've been forced off that ship, and my husband is being held against his will. So why is it that we need to have you intercede on our behalf? Your side is the one making all the claims against him. If you were to stop that, this all goes away."

"Not exactly. The allegation has been made that there are drugs, that my grandson either sells or takes drugs. And nothing could be further from the truth."

"I'm sorry, but I must object. I would like to go now, and I would like to see my husband. That's what I was promised, and that's the basis on which I got in the car with Mr. Garibaldi also."

"Oh, so he told you his name was Garibaldi?"

"That's who I was to meet."

"Well, there seems to be a little mix-up with that. And I apologize for contributing to it. Sophia, unfortunately, we are going to need to hold you here until we can secure your husband's promises and support for our cause."

"So, what you're telling me is now you're holding me? First you had my husband taken in, and now you're going to restrict me. I have children, Mr. Verasco."

"General Verasco, please."

"No, this is all wrong and I must demand that you return me to my hotel immediately. Or to the prison there. I never agreed to this, and you got me coming here under false pretenses. I don't understand what you're looking for."

"You are right about one thing, Mrs. Beale. You aren't the one we should be talking to. You are however our leverage. I'm sure that your husband will be most cooperative when he discovers this. Again, we don't wish you any harm or ill will, but my son-in-law and daughter's reputation, as well as the reputation for their son, is extremely important to us. Certain things were said that must be retracted. I'm not asking. We are demanding this as a condition of yours and your husband's freedom."

CHAPTER 18

MARK WAS PACING in his small room, inquiring every few minutes about the meeting with Sophia and the attorney. He was told continually that there had been no calls and no news. He had been allowed to make a call to Sophia's phone, but it went directly to voicemail.

He asked if one of the guards could telephone the hotel to see if she had left, and the report came back that she had been picked up and was on her way to see him with the attorney.

He knew something was wrong. She would want to be on time, she would be just as antsy to have the meeting, as he was. He called the prosecutor's cell phone and inquired.

"I'm sorry Mark, I haven't heard a thing. Let me see if I wrote the attorney's name down."

"But I understood him to be a colleague of yours. Is that not true?"

"Well, we deal with a lot of defense attorneys. I may or may not have run across him, if as you say he is a law professor, then of course he must be excellent. But honestly, I don't know the man." She shuffled some papers on her desk and then came up with a note. "Here it is, Antonio Garibaldi. Ah yes, I have heard of him. And I do believe he's a very good attorney. Would you like me to call his office?"

"Please. She is over an hour late now, and I'm concerned. Especially since she was picked up by him and isn't driving herself. I just want to make sure something hasn't happened."

"Of course. Let me call you back."

Roughly a half an hour later, Mark got the call from the prosecutor's office. "I have some bad news, and I'm going to send someone from our Naples office over to the hotel to check on the children. Sophia arranged a babysitter for them, and she left on time."

"So far so good."

"Hold on, Mr. Garibaldi had to cancel the appointment at the last minute. He had a conflict. I wasn't told this, and I don't understand why he didn't call you."

"So, who is she riding with then?" Mark asked.

"That's the thing. I don't know."

"There is absolutely nothing I can do sitting here in this room. You must understand, my wife could be in danger. I need somebody who I can trust to go check and retrace her steps. I need to know exactly where she went and who she's with if she's not with Mr. Garibaldi. Is this a kidnapping, or just a miscommunication somehow?"

"I understand fully. I will send two uniforms over to the hotel to do a welfare check. We will question the staff, and I should get some answers for you. Please, Mark, if she does show up, please call me so I don't waste unnecessary manpower."

"You got it. You know where I'll be."

It was past one o'clock in the afternoon when Mark received a call from the police station in Naples.

"Mr. Beale, your children are at the hotel, they're being watched by one of the hotel staff, they appear to be in very good shape, very happy, is there anything else we can do?"

"That's wonderful to hear. But I want to know where my wife is. She left with my new attorney, or who I thought was my new attorney, and she hasn't arrived. It's about an hour and a half past due. And that's not like her at all. This is a very important meeting, and she had to be back in Naples for another event this evening. I just don't know what's going on. Can you check the cameras and see who this person is who picked her up. Can you get a license plate?"

"Listen, Mark, we don't exactly have the resources

to check on that and you would have to file a missing or suspicious person report."

"But I'm sitting in a fucking prison in Montepulciano. I can't file that notice, and I need to know where my wife is. She could be in danger."

"I understand. Let me see what I can do, and from the communication we had with the front desk clerk, it appears she left in a white Mercedes coupe with a well-dressed individual. She appeared to know the person and left willingly. This is not a case of kidnapping."

"I understand that, but perhaps they had an accident on the way to visit me, it's not like her to be this late."

"Let's see if we can check the security cameras and get a license plate. That's the best I can do at this point. Do you have anyone else in the area you could employ to do some searching for you?"

"No, everybody on my SEAL team is back in Coronado in California. My only other friend is a ship's captain, and he is apparently docked at Capri, waiting for information on being released to continue with his itinerary, but that was the ship we were supposed to be on, and other than the captain, and my wife's elderly mother, I have no one here to rely on. Absolutely no one. Do I need to get my State Department, or the Department of Naval Affairs involved? Is this what I need to do?"

"But, at this point, it's not verified that this is a kidnapping. So, there's a limit to what we can do. But let me check with my superior and I think we can study the camera footage from the front of the hotel. And I'll re-question the desk clerk."

They had positioned Mark in the interview room, which gave him more space, and enabled him to use a phone. The prosecutor had begun to be very generous with the phone time. Mark's next call was to Teseo Dominichello. He was told that the captain was in a meeting and would return the call shortly.

Frustrated and angry, feeling that time was slipping away, he made a call to Kyle Lansdowne.

"God Mark, it's great to hear your voice. Hey, I tried to call Sophia this morning, and she doesn't pick up."

"I know Kyle. That's why I'm calling you. The attorney that you put us in touch with—"

"Garibaldi?"

"Yes. Apparently, there's been a mix up, and she was prepared to go ride with him to come up to see me and did apparently get in a car with someone she believed was Garibaldi, except that Garibaldi's office has said he had to reschedule and I'm not quite sure why we didn't get the message, but my wife has gone off with somebody else I just smell a rat. Kyle, something's wrong, I know it."

"Oh geez. I need to get hold of Teseo. Has the Department of Navy stopped by or the State Department yet?"

"I haven't seen or heard from anybody. At least they're letting me make some calls, but I'm shooting blanks here, I need to find her. And the local police say it's not a kidnapping case yet so there's a limit to what they can do. What am I supposed to do?"

"Well, I think I better call Garibaldi's office and explain what's happened. Unless they're aware of it?"

"I have no idea. I've left a message for Teseo, maybe he'll have something for me. I don't want to assume the worst, but I don't like the fact that she's been out of communication. If everything was up and up, her phone would be on, she would answer calls or make calls, she would tell me she was late and why. That makes me think they've either had an accident, or something is definitely wrong."

"God Mark, I worked on this thing halfway into the night, and I thought we had all this handled, I don't understand why the attorney's office didn't clear the schedule or make the communication but maybe they tried to and if her phone's off or lost or damaged, maybe that's what happened, but you would think they would reach out. So let me do some checking and I'll get back to you."

"Thanks Kyle. Any word from the Navy?"

"Not at this point, Mark, that's a good thing. When they start to make inquiries and get overly picky about reports and forms and all that shit, then I know something's going to hit the fan. But so far, they're kind of taking it slow. I'm hoping that they'd just like this thing to go away. But God help me Mark, I don't know what the fuck's going on. But something is throwing this whole thing off kilter. We'll get to the bottom of it. I know it sounds self-serving to say don't worry, but under the circumstances that's really all you can do is try to stay calm and know that we're doing everything we can."

"I hope somebody from state, or the Navy can jump in and overrule some of these decisions. I don't know how much leeway they have, but I need some big guns over here Kyle. And I'm losing time."

"So where are the kids?"

"They're with a staff babysitter at the Hotel Savona. I've had a welfare check on them and the police confirmed that they're happy and everything looks fine, and the hotel was aware that she was going on an appointment to see me with the attorney, and as far as they're concerned that's where she went. So, it's just that she hasn't arrived, and I've got to find out where she is."

"We'll get it done. I know you'd do the same for me. Hang in there sport. What a vacation this has been huh?"

"Don't ask me to go on a cruise. I thought third time was going to be the charm. If something happens to me on another cruise, it's because I'm a stupid dumb motherfucker and didn't listen to reason. I have no business on a boat, being a fucking dance instructor. Trying to make nice with a whole bunch of weird people. It's not my thing."

"Yeah, I know. Same thing happened to me the last time. You can't unsee some of the things you see. And if someone innocent is causing a problem, it's hard not to jump in. I get it. It's an occupational hazard for us. But I know you'd rather err on that side than on the side of not having any feelings for people or not wanting to right the wrongs that you can right. I think if it wasn't for the fact that this kid was the grandson of a cabinet minister and the son of an ambassador, it would be a whole other story. So, this one was a fluke, and how the hell did you know anyway? I'll get back to you as soon as I finish my calls."

"Thanks again Kyle."

Antonio Garibaldi showed up after three o'clock, just as the State Department representative had arrived. They sat down with Mark, listening to his story, all the bits and pieces, and now the situation with Sophia.

"You're going to have to launch a formal inquiry, Steve," Garibaldi said to the man from state. "I'm not going to be able to do that. It must come from you. And they better get their butts in gear, or it's going to be an international incident."

"I got you, let me step outside and get that going," he said.

"Mark, I need to ask you a question."

"Like I've been telling people I'm here I'm willing to cooperate, whatever you want to know just ask."

"Thanks for your patience, and frankly I'm ashamed of what's happened to you. There must be something I'm missing here because these types of things just don't happen in Italy. I mean every country has its little quirks of the judicial system, but this, this smacks of politics. And whenever politics gets involved, no matter where in the world it is, you know how that is. It fucks up everything."

"If I'd known who this kid was, maybe I would've acted differently."

"I'm not going to lecture you; you obviously know you shouldn't have pushed him up against the wall. But no way in hell should you be put through this. I'm just not sure that we're getting a fair hand here. And the fact that they're holding your wife as sort of hostage? At least that's the way it feels to me. That's way over the top. And somebody powerful is pulling some big strings, either that or they're dumb as shit. First of all, I apologize about the cancellation, I did leave a message with the front desk at the hotel for her, and I'm surprised she didn't get it."

"Well maybe that's the source of the problem. Maybe somehow that information got out to the wrong people."

"Could be, but a couple of things I need to ask you about because we have some choices on how we're going to work this. I want to bring in the news media."

"Oh no, my LPO says no media, that'll fuck it all up."

"Normally I'd agree with you, but in this case, public opinion and scrutiny in the news media, well it puts a spotlight on things and all of a sudden stuff just clears up. I think this needs to go on a local news channel, and I have a reporter friend of mine that I can leak it to, and if Steve here has lodged his complaint or inquiry, we have a reason to go to the press and ask for justice. From what I understand with the defense minister's grandson being involved in drugs, either that's a complete fabrication or completely easily disproven, or they're being dumb about this. I just think that we need some help outside of the justice system."

"You're my attorney, and I'm sorry about how you got drug into this, but I don't know whether it's a good thing or not, but I trust your instincts. You came highly recommended."

"Have the police located the person driving the Mercedes?" He asked.

"No, I haven't heard back from them."

"Okay so I'm going to have Steve ride hard on them, and I've worked with him before, and he can be a regular son of a gun. I think we need to rattle some cages; I know it's only been a day, but I sure as heck don't want this thing to go on for much longer. Suddenly, people get ideas that you're trying to throw your weight around, that the US is trying to ask for special favors for their elite warrior—we don't need any of that crap going on. You're a victim. You possibly made a little error in judgment, but you're a victim. The sooner we can get the public to understand that the better it's going to be. I'm not so sure their side is defensible in the press. I'd like to see how they squirm and how they justify it. I think that's going to tell me exactly who's behind this, and why."

"Then Mr. Garibaldi, have at it. I'll sit and talk to a reporter; I'll do whatever you want."

"No, I don't want you making any public statements, let me do that, but better still, I'd like Steve to jump in and put the weight of the United States government on their backs. We'll see what they're made from. If that doesn't work, then we'll go to plan B."

"What's plan B?" Mark asked.

"I have no fucking idea."

CHAPTER 19

SOPHIA HAD BEEN locked in the basement wine cellar of the General's estate. She was provided a sandwich, some water, and a couple of blankets and a pillow for the cot that was set up for her. She knew it was nighttime because she could hear the cicadas chirping through the foundation vents.

There was no light, until she found a small pocket flashlight on one of the tables in the storage room. It appeared they used this for bottling or labeling, and a small assembly line was set up.

She tried the door handle after she was locked inside, and found it was a lock that took a skeleton key and could be picked if she could find some strong wire. She needed to find copper wire preferably small enough so she could insert two into the keyhole.

Searching several of the shelves, she explored under papers and boxes, scoured the countertops and the two folding tables. At last, in the corner, she found some plastic-coated wiring rolled up in a coil. That required she find a pair of pliers, which she did on the bottling table. She cut herself two eight-inch strips, peeled back part of the plastic so she could insert the ends into the keyhole and with the flashlight in her mouth, was able to pick the lock very carefully.

When it at last turned over with a loud click, she was concerned that someone would hear her. With her ear up to the door, she heard music and talking, from a radio or a small TV, echoing from the kitchen area. She also previously heard pots and pans and the smell of food being prepared and assumed the General's employee was making a dinner. The cadence and movement continued, and she was grateful for the loudness of the TV.

Slowly opening the door, it emitted a loud squeak. She stopped to listen once again for any kind of activity from the kitchen. Assuming it was clear, she stepped through the doorway, closed the door quietly behind her, and tiptoed to the right down the hallway toward the front door. In the living room area, she found her purse hanging on the back of a chair and her laptop propped up against the front leg.

Slipping the laptop over her shoulder and her purse wrapped cross-body, she was able to exit the front door, scan the surrounding area and parking lot in front, and determined that no one was there, nor did there appear to be any guards. Carefully, she exited the stairway and checked both cars out, finding both locked with no sign of keys.

Her choices were to walk down the small path to the right, or head straight down the driveway toward the main road. She chose the first since she didn't want to be viewed from the second story of the house, which would be possible. It was a full moon, so the road and shrubbery glistened in the moonlight, wet with rain. She headed right.

A storage shed appeared a few feet away from the gardens surrounding the house, and with the door slightly ajar, she pried it open and found it filled with tools. Very quickly she turned on the flashlight only to get a view of what was inside and was excited to find a bicycle. Not only that, but it was also an electric bicycle, and it had been plugged in. That meant it had a full charge.

Again, securing her laptop and purse on the back of the bicycle in the basket holder, she walked it outside and realized she needed a key to turn it on. Inside she found a key that matched the brand of the bicycle hanging on a hook with a small bicycle charm on its key fob.

The bicycle whirred to life, a red light flashing and then going solid green. She mounted it and started pedaling then kicked in the electric feature. It was

quiet, and she hoped that her escape had been unde-
tected.

Sophia passed a garbage area with a dumpster, and
several recycling garbage cans next to it. There also was
a pile of leaves and garden shrubbery being composted.
The path turned slightly to the left heading more
directly to the roadway.

On her trip out to the house, she remembered
turning at a small convenience store and gas station
just before the long entrance to the estate. That's where
she headed.

Setting the bicycle around the backside of the gas
station, she tiptoed through the shadows, examining
through the windows trying to determine if someone
was in the store. A young skinny clerk with scruffy
black hair and wearing blue jeans and a Beatles T-shirt,
was perched on the stool behind the counter, watching
a small TV, smoking.

Leaving her computer case but bringing her purse,
she walked inside and greeted the store clerk. In
Italian, she asked him if she could use his telephone.

He solemnly pointed to the wall next to the freezer
compartment where there was a payphone. She asked
for change with her paper money and dialed Mark's
number. She didn't expect him to pick up, since she
was sure they had still maintained his papers, his
passport, and of course his phone and wallet.

But she was surprised.

"Hello?" Mark's warm and buttery voice was a welcome distraction. She missed him, but more than that, it was reassurance that he was not being mistreated and was healthy.

"Mark, this is Sophia. I don't have much time, but I've escaped from the General's house."

"The General? What does he have to do with this?"

"I think it was one of his men who picked me up at the hotel, impersonating the attorney, Garibaldi. I'm sorry, I was tricked, and they've been holding me here at his estate."

"Oh, my love, it is so wonderful to hear your voice. I'm here with Garibaldi right now. We were just going to be searching some addresses we found on the closed caption TVs outside the hotel. We found the license plate of the Mercedes."

"These people are looking for you to recant the story about the drugs, and his grandson. I'm going to try to ride my bicycle—"

"When did you get a bicycle?"

"Mark, just listen to me please. I don't have much time. I'm going to head down the road. I found a bicycle in the shed at the house. It's an electric bike so I should make some decent time but I'm going to head back the way he brought me, which is the opposite of traveling to Florence. I don't know what the name of the road is or the highway, but I'm just going to head back the way I remember coming."

"Gotcha."

"We turned from Naples. We were heading to Montepulciano and then he turned off toward Florence to pick up his friend he said. It turned out he brought me to the General's house, and they have kept me there since."

"That explains a lot, and oh my gosh hold on a second."

Sophia heard some conversation in the background.

"I'm about an hour and 15 minutes away Garibaldi says, so he's going to have the civil guard from Naples try to meet you on the roadway and have you wait there until I'll drive down with Garibaldi."

"So, you've been released? That's wonderful!"

"In light of what's been happening, the prosecutor decided that now is not the time to pursue charges. She would like to do a further investigation, and I'm confident she'll have everything she needs to go after these people. I am so happy you've gotten yourself free."

"Well, keep your fingers crossed, because it's dark, and the General and his henchman probably will be coming down the roadway any minute now. I'm going to be dodging in the bushes, avoiding every vehicle,

every person I see, but if they come to a little convenience store before the general's estate, they've gone too
far that means they've missed me."

"I will let them know. And thank God. I love you.
And the girls?"

"I haven't been able to talk to them, hopefully you
have."

"Not yet. But Garibaldi had the civil guard over to
watch. They did a welfare check earlier and they were
doing fine. The babysitter turned out to be a real asset.
But the police are there now, and they're waiting for
me or you. Waiting for further instructions."

"I hope I get to see you soon. I'll see you in Naples
is that correct?"

"If they don't find you in about thirty minutes, forty-five minutes perhaps, you give me back a call.
Okay?"

"Of course."

THEY HAD A tearful reunion in the Naples Police
Department. Garibaldi was introduced to Sophia, and
he turned out to be exactly the type of ally they needed.
Thank God, she thought to herself.

Mark looked great, even under the circumstances.
Sophia was exhausted, with the five-mile ride she had
gotten in by moonlight, before the police picked her
up. She was starved, so the station sprung for pizza. It

was always pizza, the universal food there.

"What's the next step?" she said folded into his arms.

"We're waiting on the prosecutor, we're waiting on Garibaldi's information, and we're also waiting for the State Department liaison who has lodged a formal inquiry as to my treatment. It's certainly going to get a lot of attention."

"I thought Kyle told us to keep it tight. He didn't want publicity."

"Garibaldi felt it was a good idea to give the story to a local reporter so we could begin to get an advance on some of the local public opinion. With the General's influence, it's possible he has friends in high places. This is going to make it more difficult for him to maneuver."

Garibaldi stepped forward. "If they are going to do illegal things, they do it in secret in the dark. They don't like the press, and our general population does not trust the government."

Sophia understood that one completely. But kept her mouth shut.

"He doesn't think the General has anything to do with the drugs, but he's trying to save his son-in-law's job. Now his own. This is a big step to foiling anything he's got up his sleeve," Mark explained.

She and Mark were free to go, and they were given

a police escort to the hotel to visit with the girls and get some rest. The local captain promised that there would be a guard placed in the hotel lobby as well as in the hallway by their room, so they would be undisturbed.

After the girls settled down, all of them wanting to climb all over Mark, hug him, kiss him, even little Domenica grabbing his lower leg and kissing his knee, which had him in stitches, they were returned to bed, and everyone settled down.

Sophia took Mark outside onto the balcony where they could view the full moon and the village lights in the distance. "You remember when we were planning this vacation?"

"Absolutely."

"I said surprise me?"

Mark grimaced and winced. "Yes."

"I don't think I'm ever going to give you that answer again. Except in bed."

CHAPTER 20

ONCE THE INVESTIGATION began, things proceeded at a record pace. Teseo was notified of their release, which relieved him greatly. Garibaldi also mentioned to him that the civil guard in Naples would be boarding the ship to escort the family of the ambassador off.

"Mark, I thank you for this. And I'd love to speak with you a little longer, but I'm going to ask for clearance to set sail. I would like to get out of Italian waters as fast as possible."

"Understood. Well, I'll let you get that done then. The civil guard should be on their way to the port now."

Teseo had docked at Naples, where there were more facilities for onboarding passengers as well as supplies for the next stage of the voyage.

"You're sure you don't want to come on board again?" the captain queried.

"No, I've been set free, but I've been told I can't leave the country yet. We're going to make sure it's all done correctly, dot every I and cross every T. And if I'm going to save my Naval career, it has to be done that way."

"So, are they going to charge the ambassador or his family?"

"My guess is no. I think the General though is in trouble."

"The General?"

"The ambassador's wife is the General's daughter. General Verasco. He's the Minister of Defense."

"Oh, I see. Yes, I would say he's in considerable trouble if he kidnapped Sophia."

"You'll be able to read a nice juicy story all about it tomorrow online. Smooth sailing, and God speed. We'll have to catch up sometime in the future. But thank you for a most memorable ten-year anniversary cruise."

"You never renewed your vows."

"Hey, it's Christmas. I'm going to do Christmas with my family. That's the most important thing of all. But second to that, my friends and allies, and the brothers I've been fortunate to serve with. I consider you one of those Teseo."

"Well, I hope your stay in Italy is uneventful now. Time for some sightseeing, maybe some good wine, and enjoy some of our fabulous food."

The hotel prepared a special breakfast for the family, since they had missed the services and the Christmas Eve dinner. Of course, neither Sophia nor Mark had done any Christmas shopping for the girls, so several of the cleaning staff as well as the front desk and the general manager, got together and wrapped some toys and children's books in Italian, and a few specialized purses and clothes for the girls. It was a different kind of Christmas than what they normally had. And Mark liked it because of its simplicity, and the fact that it didn't take them four hours to open all the packages. The girls were happy, and they were all together.

The cook made the girls special, animal-shaped pancakes done with a cookie cutter. There were delicacies from the bakery down the street, of course, the fresh espresso coffee served 24/7 in the bar, and Italian Christmas music, mostly choral groups.

After checking in with the prosecutor, and Garibaldi, Mark and Sophia and the girls decided to walk on Christmas morning down the cobblestone meandering street to the cathedral nearby. All along the way, shops displayed their finest decorations, pastries and their known specialty meats and brightly wrapped gifts.

When they got to the cathedral, the morning

church service was over, and there was a choir rehearsal, oddly, a children's choir.

"Look girls, we get to see the children's choir after all. Don't they sound beautiful?"

Domenica blurted out, "I want to."

Several members of the choir started to giggle, as Domenica's voice carried, echoing throughout the tall ceiling and balustrades.

Sophia's face and hair showed the reflection of the colorful stained-glass windows of the church, and it was fitting that on Christmas Day, they'd be sitting here together, not on a boat, not running into crazy teenagers or gossipy adults, but just being a family and listening to the joy of the holiday.

They headed out toward the narthex, to return to their hotel. The parish priest stopped them on the steps. "My children, thank you for gracing our doorway. I hope you will come back."

"Thank you, Father. We're from the States, and here on business for just a few days. But thank you for letting us listen to the beautiful choir. The girls loved it."

"It's a miracle isn't it, how all those little voices come together and make one beautiful sound?"

Mark shook his hand and then posed a question. "Do you do marriage vows? I mean redo of marriage vows?"

"Not often, not as often as I'd like to, but yes we can do that. Is it for you, my son?"

Mark looked at Sophia. "Do you want to do that today, on Christmas?"

"Are you free Father?" Sophia asked him.

"Why don't you wait and after the choir is finished, we'll do a private service for you. Would you like the girls involved?"

Neither Mark nor Sophia was able to answer since all three of the girls jumped up and down and cheered for the idea.

It was a special Christmas, a special way to celebrate ten years being together, and the family that they'd grown together, and nearly lost. It underscored to them the true meaning of Christmas, a time for the celebration of the birth of one very special child.

It was also the time to celebrate one very special family and marriage.

Did you enjoy Cruisin For Love, book 5 of the SEAL Brotherhood: Legacy series? In case you missed it, Cruisin for a SEAL, book 5 of the original SEAL Brotherhood series, is the story that introduces this couple ten years previously, where they fall in love, while battling a terrorist takeover of another cruise ship.

Stay tuned as all the original SEAL Brotherhood books are followed up with further stories in SEAL Brotherhood: Legacy series.

But if you're new to my SEALs, why don't you check out my superbundles? You can start with the first four books in the Ultimate SEAL Collection #1 or the Ultimate SEAL Collection #2, which has Cruisin For a SEAL as well as the next two books in the series.

And, as in all my SEALs and other books, nearly every story is also found on Audible, narrated by the buttery voice of my award-winning narrator, J.D. Hart.

ABOUT THE AUTHOR

 NYT and USA/Today Bestselling Author Sharon Hamilton's SEAL Brotherhood series have earned her author rankings of #1 in Romantic Suspense, Military Romance and Contemporary Romance. Her other *Brotherhood* stand-alone series are: Bad Boys of SEAL Team 3, Band of Bachelors, True Blue SEALs, Nashville SEALs, Bone Frog Brotherhood, Sunset SEALs, Bone Frog Bachelor Series and SEAL Brotherhood Legacy Series. She is a contributing author to the very popular Shadow SEALs multi-author series.

Her SEALs and former SEALs have invested in two wineries, a lavender farm and a brewery in Sonoma County, which have become part of the new stories. They also have expanded to include Veteran-benefit projects on the Florida Gulf Coast, as well as projects in Africa and the Maldives. One of the SEAL wives has even launched her own women's fiction series. But old characters, as well as children of these SEAL heroes keep returning to all the newer books.

Sharon also writes sexy paranormals in two series: Golden Vampires of Tuscany and The Guardians.

A lifelong organic vegetable and flower gardener, Sharon and her husband lived for fifty years in the Wine Country of Northern California, where many of her stories take place. Recently, they have moved to the beautiful Gulf Coast of Florida, with stories of ship-wrecks, the white sugar-sand beaches of Sunset, Treasure Island and Indian Rocks Beaches.

She loves hearing from fans through her website: authorsharonhamilton.com

Find out more about Sharon, her upcoming releases, appearances and news when you sign up for Sharon's newsletter.

Facebook:
facebook.com/SharonHamiltonAuthor

Twitter:
twitter.com/sharonlhamilton

Pinterest:
pinterest.com/AuthorSharonH

Amazon:
amazon.com/Sharon-Hamilton/e/B004FQQMAC

BookBub:
bookbub.com/authors/sharon-hamilton

Youtube:
youtube.com/channel/UCDInkxXFpXp_4Vnq08ZxMBQ

Soundcloud:
soundcloud.com/sharon-hamilton-1

Sharon Hamilton's Rockin' Romance Readers:
facebook.com/groups/sealteamromance

Sharon Hamilton's Goodreads Group:
goodreads.com/group/show/199125-sharon-hamilton-readers-group

Visit Sharon's Online Store:
sharon-hamilton-author.myshopify.com

Join Sharon's Review Teams:

eBook Reviews:
sharonhamiltonassistant@gmail.com

Audio Reviews:
sharonhamiltonassistant@gmail.com

Life *is one fool thing after another.*
Love *is two fool things after each other.*

REVIEWS

"An excellent paranormal romance that was exciting, romantic, entertaining and very satisfying to read. It had me anticipating what would happen next many times over, so much so I could not put it down and even finished it up in a day. The vampires in this book were different from your average vampire, but I enjoy different variations and changes to the same old stuff. It made for a more unpredictable read and more adventurous to explore! Vampire lovers, any paranormal readers and even those who love the romance genre will enjoy Honeymoon Bite."

"This is the first non-Seal book of this author's I have read and I loved it. There is a cast-like hierarchy in this vampire community with humans at the very bottom and Golden vampires at the top. Lionel is a dark vampire who are servants of the Goldens. Phoebe is a Golden who has not decided if she will remain human or accept the turning to become a vampire. Either way she and Lionel can never be together since it is forbidden.

I enjoyed this story and I am looking forward to the next installment."

"A hauntingly romantic read. Old love lost and new love found. Family, heart, intrigue and vampires. Grabbed my attention and couldn't put down. Would definitely recommend."

PRAISE FOR THE
SEAL BROTHERHOOD SERIES

"Fans of Navy SEAL romance, I found a new author to feed your addiction. Finely written and loaded delicious with moments, Sharon Hamilton's storytelling satisfies like a thick bar of chocolate." —Marliss Melton, bestselling author of the *Team Twelve* Navy SEALs series

"Sharon Hamilton does an EXCELLENT job of fitting all the characters into a brotherhood of SEALS that may not be real but sure makes you feel that you have entered the circle and security of their world. The stories intertwine with each book before…and each book after and THAT is what makes Sharon Hamilton's SEAL Brotherhood Series so very interesting. You won't want to put down ANY of her books and they will keep you reading into the night when you should be sleeping. Start with this book…and you will not want to stop until you've read the whole series and then…you will be waiting for Sharon to write the next one." (5 Star Review)

"Kyle and Christy explode all over the pages in this first book, *[Accidental SEAL],* in a whole new series of SEALs. If the twist and turns don't get your heart jumping, then maybe the suspense will. This is a must read for those that are looking for love and adventure with a little sloppy love thrown in for good measure." (5 Star Review)

PRAISE FOR THE
BAD BOYS OF SEAL TEAM 3 SERIES

"I love reading this series! Once you start these books, you can hardly put them down. The mix of romance and suspense keeps you turning the pages one right after another! Can't wait until the next book!" (5 Star Review)

"I love all of Sharon's Seal books, but *[SEAL's Code]* may just be her best to date. Danny and Luci's journey is filled with a wonderful insight into the Native American life. It is a love story that will fill you with warmth and contentment. You will enjoy Danny's journey to become a SEAL and his reasons for it. Good job Sharon!" (5 Star Review)

PRAISE FOR THE
BAND OF BACHELORS SERIES

"*[Lucas]* was the first book in the Band of Bachelors series and it was a phenomenal start. I loved how we got to see the other SEALs we all love and we got a look at Lucas and Marcy. They had an instant attraction, and their love was very intense. This book had it all, suspense, steamy romance, humor, everything you want in a riveting, outstanding read. I can't wait to read the next book in this series." (5 Star Review)

PRAISE FOR THE
TRUE BLUE SEALS SERIES

"Keep the tissues box nearby as you read *True Blue SEALs: Zak* by Sharon Hamilton. I imagine more than I wish to that the circumstances surrounding Zak and Amy are all too real for returning military personnel and their families. Ms. Hamilton has put us right in the middle of struggles and successes that these two high school sweethearts endure. I have read several of Sharon Hamilton's military romances but will say this is the most emotionally intense of the ones that I have read. This is a well-written, realistic story with authentic characters that will have you rooting for them and proud of those who serve to keep us safe. This is an author who writes amazing stories that you love and cry with the characters. Fans of Jessica Scott and Marliss Melton will want to add Sharon Hamilton to their list of realistic military romance writers." (5 Star Review)

"Dear FATHER IN HEAVEN,

If I may respectfully say so sometimes you are a strange God. Though you love all mankind,

It seems you have special predilections too.

You seem to love those men who can stand up alone who face impossible odds, Who challenge every bully and every tyrant ~

Those men who know the heat and loneliness of Calvary. Possibly you cherish men of this stamp because you recognize the mark of your only son in them.

Since this unique group of men known as the SEALs know Calvary and suffering, teach them now the mystery of the resurrection ~ that they are indestructible, that they will live forever because of their deep faith in you.

And when they do come to heaven, may I respectfully warn you, Dear Father, they also know how to celebrate. So please be ready for them when they insert under your pearly gates.

Bless them, their devoted Families and their Country on this glorious occasion.

We ask this through the merits of your Son, Christ Jesus the Lord, Amen."

By Reverend E.J. McMalhon S.J. LCDR, CHC, USN
Awards Ceremony SEAL Team One
1975 At NAB, Coronado

Made in the USA
Coppell, TX
15 December 2022

89307288R00138